DIVIDED LOYALTY

The captain's eyes came to rest on the barns. "You've got horses in those stalls?"

"Yes, but—"

"I'd like to see them," Captain Denton said, spurring his own flagging mount forward.

Ruff grabbed his bit. "Hold up there, Captain, you haven't been invited."

"And since when does an officer of the Confederacy need to beg permission for horses so that your countrymen can live according to our own laws?"

"*I'm* the law on this place," Justin thundered. "And my mares are in foal. They're not going to war, Captain. These are Thoroughbred horses, sir! Horses bred to race."

"The race," Denton said through clenched teeth, "is to see if we can bring relief to our men who are, this very moment, fighting on Lookout Mountain and Missionary Ridge. Our boys are dying, Mr. Ballou. Dying for the right to determine the South's great destiny. But maybe your attitude has a lot to do with why you married a Cherokee woman."

Something snapped behind Justin Ballou's obsidian eyes. He would have broken the Confederate captain's neck if his sons had not broken his stranglehold. . . .

THE HORSEMEN

GARY McCARTHY

DIAMOND BOOKS, NEW YORK

THE HORSEMEN

A Diamond Book / published by arrangement with
the author

PRINTING HISTORY
Diamond edition / June 1992

ISBN: 1-55773-733-9

Diamond Books are published by The Berkley Publishing
Group, 200 Madison Avenue, New York, New York 10016.
The name "DIAMOND" and its logo are trademarks
belonging to Charter Communications, Inc.

PRINTED IN THE UNITED STATES OF AMERICA

10 9 8 7 6 5 4 3 2 1

ONE

November 24, 1863—Just east of Chattanooga, Tennessee

The chestnut stallion's head snapped up very suddenly. Its nostrils quivered, then flared, testing the wind, tasting the approach of unseen danger. Old Justin Ballou's watchful eye caught the stallion's motion and he also froze, senses focused. For several long moments, man and stallion remained motionless, and then Justin Ballou opened the gate to the paddock and limped toward the tall Thoroughbred. He reached up and his huge, blue-veined hand stroked the stallion's muzzle. "What is it, High Man?" he asked softly. "What now, my friend?"

In answer, the chestnut dipped its head several times and stamped its feet with increasing nervousness. Justin began to speak soothingly to the stallion, his deep, resonant voice flowing like a mystical incantation. Almost at once, the stallion grew calm. After a few minutes, Justin said, as if to an old and very dear friend, "Is it one of General Grant's Union patrols this time, High Man? Have they come to take what little I have left? If so, I will gladly fight them to the death."

The stallion shook its head, rolled its eyes, and snorted as if it could smell Yankee blood. Justin's thick fingers scratched a special place behind the stallion's ear. The chestnut lowered its head to nuzzle the man's chest.

"Don't worry. It's probably another Confederate patrol," Justin said thoughtfully. "But what can they want this time? I have already given them three fine sons and most of your offspring. There is so little left to give—but they know that! Surely they can see my empty stalls and paddocks."

Justin turned toward the road leading past his neat, whitewashed fences that sectioned and cross-sectioned his famous Tennessee horse ranch, known throughout the South as Wildwood Farm. The paddocks were empty and silent. There were no proud mares with their colts, and no prancing fillies to bless the old man's vision or give him the joy he'd known for so many years. It was the war—this damned killing Civil War. "No more!" Justin cried. "You'll have no more of my fine horses or sons!"

The stallion spun and galloped away. High Man was seventeen years old, long past his prime, but he and a few other Ballou-bred stallions still sired the fastest and handsomest horses in the South. Just watching the chestnut run made Justin feel a little better. High Man was a living testimony to the extraordinarily fine care he'd received all these years at Wildwood Farm. No one would believe that at his ripe age he could still run and kick his heels up like a three-year-old colt.

The stallion ran with such fluid grace that he seemed to float across the earth. When the Thoroughbred reached the far end of the paddock, it skidded to a sliding stop, chest banging hard against the fence. It spun around, snorted, and shook its head for an expected shout of approval.

But not this day. Instead, Justin made himself leave the paddock, chin up, stride halting but resolute. He could hear thunder growing louder. Could it be the sound of cannon from as far away as the heights that General Bragg and his Rebel army now held in wait of the Union army's expected assault? No, the distance was too great even to carry the roar of heavy artillery. That told Justin that his initial hunch was correct and the sound growing in his ears had to be racing hoofbeats.

But were they enemy or friend? Blue coat or gray? Justin planted his big work boots solidly in the dust of the country road; either way, he would meet them.

"Father!"

He recognized his fourteen-year-old daughter's voice and ignored it, wanting Dixie to stay inside their mansion. Justin drew a pepperbox pistol from his waistband. If this actually was a dreaded Union cavalry patrol, then someone was going to die this afternoon. A man could only be pushed so far and then he had to fight.

"Father!" Dixie's voice was louder now, more strident. "Father!"

Justin reluctantly twisted about to see his daughter and her oldest brother, Houston, running toward him. Both had guns clenched in their fists.

"Who is it!" Houston gasped, reaching Justin first and trying to catch his wind.

Justin did not dignify the stupid question with an answer. In a very few minutes, they would know. "Dixie, go back to the house."

"Please, I . . . I just can't!"

"Dixie! Do as Father says," Houston stormed. "This is no time for arguing. Go to the house!"

Dixie's black eyes sparked. She stood her ground. Houston was twenty-one and a man full grown, but he was still just her big brother. "I'm staying."

Houston's face darkened with anger and his knuckles whitened as he clutched the gun in his fist. "Dammit, you heard . . ."

"Quiet, the both of you!" Justin commanded. "Here they come."

A moment later a dust-shrouded patrol lifted from the earth to come galloping up the road.

"It's *our* boys," Dixie yelped with relief. "It's a Reb patrol!"

"Yeah," Houston said, taking an involuntary step forward, "but they been shot up all to hell!"

Justin slipped his gun back into his waistband and was seized by a flash of dizziness. Dixie moved close, steadying him until the spell passed a moment later. "You all right?"

Justin nodded. He did not know what was causing the dizziness, but the spells seemed to come often these days. No doubt, it was the war. This damned war that the South was steadily losing. And the death of two of his five strapping sons and . . .

Houston had stepped out in front and now he turned to shout, "Mason is riding with them!"

Justin's legs became solid and strong again. Mason was the middle son, the short, serious one that wanted to go into medicine and who read volumes of poetry despite the teasing from his brothers.

Dixie slipped her gun into the pocket of the loose-fitting pants she insisted on wearing around the horses. She glanced up at her father and said, "Mason will be hungry and so will the others. They'll need food and bandaging."

"They'll have both," Justin declared without hesitation, "but no more of my Thoroughbreds!"

"No more," Dixie vowed. "Mason will understand."

"Yeah," Houston said, coming back to stand by his father, "but the trouble is, he isn't in charge. That's a captain he's riding alongside."

Justin was about to speak, but from the corner of his eye, saw a movement. He twisted, hand instinctively lifting the pepperbox because these woods were crawling with both Union and Confederate deserters, men often half-crazy with fear and hunger.

"Pa, don't you dare shoot me!" Rufus "Ruff" Ballou called, trying to force a smile as he moved forward, long and loose-limbed with his rifle swinging at his side.

"Ruff, what the hell you doing hiding in those trees!" Houston demanded, for he too had been startled enough to raise his gun.

If Ruff noticed the heat in his older brother's voice, he chose to ignore it.

"Hell, Houston, I was just hanging back a little to make sure these were friendly visitors."

"It's Mason," Justin said, turning back to the patrol. "And from the looks of these boys, things are going from bad to worse."

There were just six men in the patrol, two officers and four enlisted. One of the enlisted was bent over nearly double with pain, a blossom of red spreading across his left shoulder. Two others were riding double on a runty sorrel.

"That sorrel is gonna drop if it don't get feed and rest," Ruff observed, his voice hardening with disapproval.

"All of their mounts look like they've been chased to hell and back without being fed or watered," Justin stated. "We'll make sure they're watered and grained before these boys leave."

The Ballous nodded. It never occurred to any of them that a horse should ever leave their farm in worse shape then when it had arrived. The welfare of livestock just naturally came first—even over their own physical needs.

Justin stepped forward and raised his hand in greeting. Deciding that none of the horses were in desperate circumstances, he fixed his attention on Mason. He was shocked. Mason was a big man, like his father and brothers, but now he appeared withered—all ridges and angles. His cap was missing and his black hair was wild and unkempt. His cheeks were hollow, and the sleeve of his right arm had been cut away, and now his arm was wrapped in a dirty bandage. The loose, sloppy way he sat his horse told Justin more eloquently than words how weak and weary Mason had become after just eight months of fighting the armies of the North.

The patrol slowed to a trot, then a walk, and Justin saw the captain turn to speak to Mason. Justin couldn't hear the words, but he could see by the senior officer's expression that the man was angry and upset. Mason rode trancelike, eyes fixed on his family, lips a thin, hard slash instead of the expected smile of greeting.

Mason drew his horse to a standstill before his father and brothers. Up close, his appearance was even more shocking.

"Mason?" Justin whispered when his son said nothing. "Mason, are you all right?"

Mason blinked. Shook himself. "Father. Houston. Ruff. Dixie. You're all looking well. How are the horses?"

"What we got left are fine," Justin said cautiously. "Only a few on the place even fit to run. Sold all the fillies and colts last fall. But you knew that."

"You did the right thing to keep Houston and Ruff out of this," Mason said.

Houston and Ruff took a sudden interest in the dirt under their feet. The two youngest Ballou brothers had desperately wanted to join the Confederate army, but Justin had demanded that they remain at Wildwood Farm, where they could help carry on the family business of raising Thoroughbreds. Only now, instead of racetracks and cheering bettors, the Ballou horses swiftly carried messages between the generals of the Confederate armies. Many times the delivery of a vital message depended on horses with pure blazing speed.

"Lieutenant," the captain said, clearing his throat loudly, "I think this chatter has gone on quite long enough. Introduce me."

Mason flushed with humiliation. "Father, allow me to introduce Captain Denton."

Justin had already sized up the captain, and what he saw did not please him. Denton was a lean, straight-backed man. He rode as if he had a rod up his ass and he looked like a mannequin glued to the saddle. He was an insult to the fine tradition of Southern cavalry officers.

"Captain," Justin said without warmth, "if you'll order your patrol to dismount, we'll take care of your wounded and these horses."

"Private Wilson can't ride any farther," Denton said. "And there isn't time for rest."

"But you *have* to," Justin argued. "These horses are—"

"Finished," Denton said. "We must have replacements, that's why we are here, Mr. Ballou."

Justin paled ever so slightly. "Hate to tell you this, Captain, but I'm afraid you're going to be disappointed. I've already given all the horses I can to the Confederacy— sons, too."

Denton wasn't listening. His eyes swept across the paddock.

"What about *that* one," he said, pointing toward High Man. "He looks to be in fine condition."

"He's past his racing prime," Houston argued. "He's our foundation sire now and is used strictly for breeding."

"Strictly for breeding?" Denton said cryptically. "Mr. Ballou, there is not a male creature on this earth who would not like to—"

"Watch your tongue, sir!" Justin stormed. "My daughter's honor will not be compromised!"

Captain Denton's eyes jerked sideways to Dixie and he blushed. Obviously, he had not realized Dixie was a girl with her baggy pants and a felt slouch hat pulled down close to her eyebrows.

"My sincere apologies." The captain dismissed her and his eyes came to rest on the barns. "You've got horses in those stalls?"

"Yes, but—"

"I'd like to see them," Denton said, spurring his own flagging mount forward.

Ruff grabbed his bit. "Hold up there, Captain, you haven't been invited."

"And since when does an officer of the Confederacy need to beg permission for horses so that *your* countrymen, as well as mine, can live according to our own laws!"

"*I'm* the law on this place," Justin thundered. "And my mares are in foal. They're not going to war, Captain. Neither they nor the last of my stallions are going to be chopped to pieces on some battlefield or have their legs ruined while trying to pull supply wagons. These are *Thoroughbred* horses, sir! Horses bred to race."

"The race," Denton said through clenched teeth, "is to see if we can bring relief to our men who are, this very moment, fighting on Lookout Mountain and Missionary Ridge."

Denton's voice shook with passion. "The plundering armies of General Ulysses Grant, General George Thomas, and his Army of the Cumberland are attacking our soldiers right now, and God help me if I've ever seen such slaughter! Our boys are dying, Mr. Ballou! Dying for the right to determine the South's great destiny. We—not you and your piddling horses—are making the ultimate sacrifices! But maybe your attitude has a lot to do with why you married a Cherokee Indian woman."

Something snapped behind Justin Ballou's obsidian eyes. He saw the faces of his two oldest sons, one reported to have been blown to pieces by a Union battery in the battle of Bull Run and the other trampled to death in a bloody charge at Shiloh. Their proud mother's Cherokee blood had made them the first in battle and the first in death.

Justin lunged, liver-spotted hands reaching upward. Too late Captain Denton saw murder in the old man's eyes. He tried to rein his horse off, but Justin's fingers clamped on his coat and his belt. With a tremendous heave, Denton was torn from his saddle and hurled to the ground. Justin growled like a huge dog as his fingers crushed the breath out of Denton's life.

He would have broken the Confederate captain's neck if his sons had not broken his stranglehold. Two of the mounted soldiers reached for their pistols, but Ruff's own rifle made them freeze and then slowly raise their hands.

"Pa!" Mason shouted, pulling Justin off the nearly unconscious officer. "Pa, stop it!"

As suddenly as it had flared, Justin's anger died, and

he had to be helped to his feet. He glared down at the wheezing cavalry officer and his voice trembled when he said, "Captain Denton, I don't know how the hell you managed to get a commission in Jeff Davis's army, but I do know this: lecture me about sacrifice for the South again and I will break your fool neck! Do you hear me!"

The captain's eyes mirrored raw animal fear. "Lieutenant Ballou," he choked at Mason, "I *order* you in the name of the Army of the Confederacy to confiscate fresh horses!"

"Go to hell."

"I'll have you court-martialed and shot for insubordination!"

Houston drew his pistol and aimed it at Denton's forehead. "Maybe you'd better change your tune, Captain."

"No!"

Justin surprised them all by coming to Denton's defense. "If you shoot him—no matter how much he deserves to be shot—our family will be judged traitors."

"But . . ."

"Put the gun away," Justin ordered wearily. "I'll give him fresh horses."

"Pa!" Ruff cried. "What are you going to give to him? Our mares?"

"Yes, but not all of them. Just the youngest and the strongest. And those matched three-year-old stallions you and Houston are training."

"But, Pa," Ruff protested, "they're just green broke."

"I know, but this will season them in a hurry," Justin said levelly. "Besides, there's no choice. High Man leaves Wildwood Farm over my dead body."

"Yes, sir," Ruff said, knowing his father was not running a bluff.

Dixie turned away in anger and started toward the house. "I'll see we get food cooking for the soldiers and some fresh bandages for Private Wilson."

A moment later, Ruff stepped over beside the wounded

soldier. "Here, let me give you a hand down. We'll go up to the house and take a look at that shoulder."

Wilson tried to show his appreciation as both Ruff and Houston helped him to dismount. "Much obliged," he whispered. "Sorry to be of trouble."

Mason looked to his father. "Sir, I'll take responsibility for your horses."

"How can you do that?" Houston demanded of his brother. "These three-year-old stallions and our mares will go crazy amid all that cannon and rifle fire. No one but us can control them. It would be—"

"Then you and Ruff need to come on back with us," Mason said.

"No!" Justin raged. "I paid for their replacements! I've got the papers saying that they can't be drafted or taken into the Confederate army."

"Maybe not," Mason said, "but they can volunteer to help us save lives up on the mountains where General Bragg is in danger of being overrun, and where our boys are dying for lack of medical attention."

"No!" Justin choked. "I've given too much already!"

"Pa, we won't fight. We'll just go to handle the horses." Ruff placed his hand on his father's shoulder. "No fighting," he pledged, looking past his father at the road leading toward Chattanooga and the battlefields. "I swear it."

Justin shook his head, not believing a word of it. His eyes shifted from Mason to Houston and finally settled on Ruff. "You boys are *fighters*! Oh, I expect you'll even try to do as you promised, but you won't be able to once you smell gunpowder and death. You'll fight and get yourselves killed, just like Micha and John."

Mason shook his head vigorously. "Pa, I swear that once the horses are delivered and hitched to those ambulances and supply wagons, I'll send Houston and Ruff back to you. All right?"

After a long moment, Justin finally managed to nod his

head. "Come along," he said to no one in particular, "we'll get our Thoroughbreds ready."

But Captain Denton's thin lips twisted in anger. "I want a *dozen* horses! Not one less will do. And I still want that big chestnut stallion in that paddock for my personal mount."

Houston scoffed with derision, "Captain, I've seen some fools in my short lifetime, but none as big as you."

"At least," Denton choked, "my daddy didn't buy my way out of the fighting."

Houston's face twisted with fury and his hand went for the Army Colt strapped to his hip. It was all that Ruff could do to keep his older brother from gunning down the ignorant cavalry officer.

"You *are* a fool," Ruff gritted at the captain when he'd calmed Houston down. "And if you should be lucky enough to survive this war, you'd better pray that you never come across me or any of my family."

Denton wanted to say something. His mouth worked but Ruff's eyes told him he wouldn't live long enough to finish even a single sentence, so the captain just clamped his mouth shut and spun away in a trembling rage.

TWO

Dixie's mother had died six years earlier while away helping her Cherokee people during a cholera epidemic in the Great Smoky Mountains of North Carolina. Most of the Cherokee had been driven far to the Oklahoma Territory long before, during the terrible time now referred to as the "Trail of Tears." Only about three hundred had escaped the army's grasp and, vowing to die rather than be taken from their mountains, had escaped relocation to hide in the Smokies.

One of the Cherokee fugitive leaders had been called Tasali. When Tasali had fought and killed a soldier to defend his own life, he had fled to the forests and could not be captured. Anxious to make an example of the Indian leader, the United States Army had agreed that, if Tasali surrendered, his rebel band would not be hunted down, persecuted, and sent to Oklahoma. Tasali had soon presented himself to the army authorities. He was sentenced without justice, then publicly executed, but his name had become legend among the Cherokee. Dixie could still recall how her mother had spoken Tasali's name with great pride.

Her mother's maiden name had been Lucinda Eldee Starr and her Cherokee name had been Ah-na-hi Noxie. Dixie remembered her mother as tall, quiet, and very graceful. Lucinda had not been one to giggle or laugh much, but from what Dixie learned from her older brothers and those who remembered her more clearly, her mother had been a happy woman.

There were several old daguerreotypes of Lucinda Starr in the house, and although the Cherokee woman had refused to smile before a camera, Dixie thought she saw a twinkle in her mother's dark eyes. The pictures brought back very dim memories of her mother singing songs in both Cherokee and English. Lucinda Starr had been a mixed-blood Cherokee and her family had once had a large cotton plantation and slaves in North Carolina. But all that had been lost during the constant relocations endured by the Cherokee people.

Now, as Dixie scurried about her household helping with the preparations for a large meal for their unexpected soldier guests, she heard the front door bang shut. Dixie wiped perspiration from her brow with her sleeve and walked quickly down the marble-floored hallway. Though fourteen, she was already taller than most women at five feet six, but her figure was slim and boyish. Perhaps if she did not spend so much of her time riding and working around horses, she would have been more developed. Dixie did not care. Everyone on Wildwood Farm knew that horses—not boys—were her passion.

Dixie saw that Houston and Ruff were helping the badly wounded young Confederate cavalryman inside.

"Bring him upstairs into the blue guest room," she said, leading the way up a winding marble stairway to the upper landing.

Their home had eight bedrooms, five on the top floor and three on the bottom. The blue guest room was always held ready to receive horse buyers who frequently visited Wildwood in the hope of purchasing a prized Thoroughbred. Most often, these buyers went away disappointed because Justin was very selective about who could have his horses. The Ballou bloodline was his life's work. He had developed it over thirty years of continual trial and error, always seeking to breed not only the fastest racehorses that ever graced a Southern track, but also horses strong of bone so that they would not break down after a few racing seasons and then have to be destroyed. At Wildwood, if a stallion went lame but its nerves could be deadened by hot plasters, then it could be spared for breeding or gelded and gentled to be a carriage or even a lady's horse. Mares, of course, were for admiring, fussing with, and breeding. Justin prized them as much as an Arabian king would treasure his harem. He called them his "girls" and he brought them presents of sugar and flowers, especially after they presented him with a brand-new foal.

At Wildwood, it was often only half-jokingly suggested that *horses* were the real guests of honor. Dixie knew her father held that to be the truth.

"Strip off your shirt, Private."

The young man turned at the sound of Dixie's voice. His eyes were feverish and dulled with pain. He blinked at Dixie and it was clear that he did not understand.

Houston and Ruff tried to be gentle removing his shirt, but the dried blood made it slow, painful work. Despite their best efforts, it must have been extremely painful when the wound reopened and began to bleed.

"Is the bullet out yet?" Houston asked. Ruff shook his head. "I don't see any sign that this poor fella has been doctored."

"I'll get some sour mash and we'll see if we can get a bottle poured down his throat before we start digging," Dixie said.

Her two brothers nodded in agreement, and it took only a moment for Dixie to return with a bottle of her father's liquor.

"Open your mouth," Ruff ordered.

The private stared dully at him until Houston pinched a thumb and forefinger into his cheeks so hard that his mouth opened. At the same moment, Dixie jammed the bottle into the soldier's mouth, and while Ruff pinched the soldier's lips tight around the bottle and bent his head back, Dixie poured.

The soldier choked and sputtered something awful, but he got the liquor down. Dixie and her brothers had helped doctor injured men and horses from their earliest memories, and now that Justin's eyes were not as clear or his fingers as nimble, they had taken over that responsibility. They had surgical kits both inside the house and out in the barn for emergencies. Justin did not believe in making man or beast suffer in wait for a doctor or veterinarian to sashay out from Chattanooga.

"You want to do it?" Ruff asked his older brother as he opened the medical kit and laid out the scalpel, forceps, needle, suture, and a few other surgical supplies.

"Sure," Houston said, removing his hat, rolling up his sleeves and saying, "Ruff, you pin him down as best you can. Dixie, you help with the bandages and be ready with a needle and suture."

With that, Houston, who possessed hands almost too graceful for a man, took up the scalpel and made a deep, inch-long incision across the wound.

"Ahhhh!" the private screamed, coming off the table, fighting Ruff, who, although very powerful, had his hands full.

"Try to hold his legs down!" Houston snapped, grabbing up bandages and swiping at the incision so that he could see well enough to make a crosscut.

Again, the soldier cried out and bucked. Ruff grunted, "Damn, he's too skinny to be this strong."

"He's suffering," Dixie gritted, leaning on the man's legs and trying to keep them from kicking her across the room.

With his fine hands, Houston was as adept with the scalpel and the forceps as he was with a deck of cards. Dixie envied his cool nerve as Houston jammed the clumsy forceps into the festering bullet hole and then closed his eyes, every ounce of his concentration on the steel in his fingers.

The bleeding was coming much faster now, which was a good sign, for this would cleanse the wound, but bad because the soldier had probably already lost too much blood.

"Feel the bullet yet?" Dixie asked.

"If I did, I'd be latching on to it and pulling it out!" Houston snapped. "Now *shhh*! I can't answer fool questions and concentrate on this at the same time."

Stung by her brother's sharp rebuke, Dixie seethed. Houston could be a real son of a bitch but you had to admire him. He was tough and decisive and more like her father than any of her other brothers. Had Houston been allowed to join the Confederate army, he'd have died quite gloriously in his very first cavalry charge. Justin knew that, and for that very same reason fought so hard to keep Houston on the farm.

"There!" Houston said, eyes snapping open. "Got it!"

They watched as he started to retract the forceps from the wound, but suddenly he cussed. Dixie knew then that he had lost the bullet and, to her surprise, Houston withdrew the forceps and plunged his thumb and forefinger into the wound. The private fainted.

"It'll be too slippery to get out that way!" Ruff argued.

Houston wasn't listening and maybe it was because he figured he could extract the spent bullet just fine.

"Come on, come on!"

An instant later, Houston extracted the offending bullet. He carefully wiped it clean and then held it up for everyone to inspect. The slug was flattened and misshapen. Houston shook his head. "I'm afraid it tore up his shoulder."

Ruff agreed. "He'll still be able to use it some, but it'll probably never be strong again."

Dixie cleansed the wound with the same powerful medicine they used on their horses, and then began to suture.

"I can handle the rest of this," Dixie said. "Why don't you both go and make sure that neither Father nor Mason kills that fool captain."

Ruff nodded with agreement but, before leaving, he said, "You do nice stitches, Dixie. If that boy lives, he'll appreciate your needlework."

Dixie allowed him a smile. Ruff was her favorite brother.

They had always been close age-wise and otherwise. Ruff was also the best horseman of her brothers, though he was inclined to be a little too lenient with an obstreperous horse. If not watched, he could even spoil them.

After her brothers had gone, Dixie was able to hear the house servants as they went outside with food for the Confederate soldiers. The cavalrymen would be fed at a long oak table under a huge elm tree. They'd have cold buttermilk, bread, and slices of both sugar ham and chicken. Unless Dixie missed her guess, there would also be apple and custard pie. The cavalrymen would think they had died and gone to heaven after their tiresome army fare of beans and hardtack.

When the suturing was finished, Dixie cleaned up the young man, frequently studying his pale face. She wondered what his name might be and where in the South he had grown up. Dixie also wondered if this young private had brothers and sisters. It seemed very likely that this boy had family thinking of him and praying for his safety this very minute, just as she had prayed for John and Micha— until the news arrived, informing her of their deaths on the battlefields of Bull Run and Shiloh.

And now there was reason to pray for Mason every day. What a surprise it had been to see him. But he was so thin, and there was great sadness in his eyes. . . .

Dixie turned away from the unconscious young soldier. How she hated this terrible war! And despite endlessly hearing about it, she confessed that she still couldn't understand why intelligent men could not just sit down and settle their differences peaceably. Or if they couldn't do that, then let each side pick a champion and, like David and Goliath, let the two of them settle the issue. Wasn't that much better than losing thousands in a struggle that seemed as if it would never end? The last time that Dixie visited Chattanooga, her expectancy had turned into sadness when she saw all the maimed young soldiers hanging around the courthouse, the city park, and the armory. There had been none of the excitement she'd seen after the first and second great Confederate victories at Bull Run. After thirty-one hellish months of war, General Ulysses S. Grant seemed unstoppable. Nashville, Vicksburg. New Orleans. All these beloved Southern cities and more had fallen. Now, Dixie could feel the South in pain. Food, clothing, armaments, and even hope were almost all gone. It was an awful thing to look at those maimed soldiers and see in their vacant stares that they knew their sacrifice might well be in vain.

"Dixie?"

She turned to see her father and Captain Denton. "Yes?"

Justin's lined face looked very old and grim. "Captain Denton wishes a report on his wounded private."

"He's doing well," Dixie said with as much civility as she could muster. "He'll survive but without the full use of that arm and shoulder."

Denton removed his hat. His hair was quite thin, and Dixie noted that his throat was already discolored where her father had grabbed and choked him. "Miss Ballou, I am sorry about that little mistake I made outside. As you can well imagine, I was upset and—"

"What shall we do with your private when he is well enough to travel?" Dixie interrupted.

Denton's cheeks reddened. "Tell him to report to the nearest Confederate army. I can't say where that might be."

"Very well."

Dixie turned to her father. "Are our mares ready to be sent to their slaughter?"

"Dixie!"

The moment the words had passed from her lips, Dixie regretted them because she knew her father did not hold much hope of ever seeing these horses again, either. "I'm sorry, Father."

Captain Denton replaced his cap. "You have a great deal to learn, Miss Ballou."

It was Dixie's turn to feel anger. "At least I am aware of the fact."

The captain spun on his heel and hurried outside. Justin, however, waited behind a moment, eyes locked with those of his only daughter.

"I said I was sorry, Father. I meant it. And I'm sure, with Ruff and Houston taking care of those mares, that everything will be all right."

"Your mother didn't have a sharp tongue," Justin said wearily. "If you were a man and said the things you do, I'm afraid that you'd often be challenged to a duel or knife fight."

"If I were a man, I wouldn't be expected to suffer such fools as that captain."

Her father actually smiled. "Yes you would, Dixie. We all have to. Look at Mason and what he is going through in order to serve the Confederacy."

"It's a mistake," Dixie said bitterly. "This whole damn war is just one terrible mistake!"

"The bigger mistake," Justin said, "is not to be willing to fight or die for what we believe. So, do I believe that the South should choose her own destiny? The answer will always be yes."

Dixie felt a rush of shame. She hugged her father and looked up into his suffering eyes. "I believe in *you*, Father. And in honor and in the beauty of the South. And in our horses and in God. I believe in all those things and more. I believe in life, too!"

He nodded. "This war will pass, as it must. And then, no matter what is left of the South, she *will* live!"

"I'm glad, Father," Dixie said. "Now, you'd better go back out and make sure the captain doesn't push Mason, Houston, or Ruff over the brink and get himself killed."

"Good idea."

"Father?"

He stopped in the doorway. "Yes?"

"Is it so terrible for a girl to say what is on her mind?

To be as honest and straightforward as a man?"

Justin frowned. "It shouldn't be," he said at last. "But like it or not, you are going to be a Southern lady. That means you must always act like one."

"I don't think I can."

"Try," Justin said, heavily. "That's all I'll ever ask of you."

Dixie stayed with the private until she heard the captain's shouted command for his patrol to mount up in formation. She hurried out on the wide veranda, and her heart sank to see the Ballou mares roped together like slaves. Every horse raised on Wildwood was gently and patiently broken to ride, but the mares seldom had to do anything except bear their foals. Now they looked rather dowdy and pathetic as they prepared to be led off to war.

Mason saw her and waved good-bye, but Ruff and Houston, riding the last few of their precious stallions, did not look to either side. Their faces were grim and they were heavily armed.

Godspeed you and the mares home soon, Dixie prayed. And you too, Mason. In fact, Godspeed all of you back to your homes and families, even that fool, Captain Denton.

As if he sensed her prayer for him, the captain turned and stared at her just before he rounded the bend.

THREE

Ruff Ballou shifted his rifle on his lap and rode stirrup to stirrup with his brothers up the dusty road toward Chattanooga. He had been this way a thousand times before but never had he felt so twisted up with nerves as he did right now. There was a battle raging just up ahead; Ruff knew that much as well as the military events that had led up to this very day.

In this autumn of 1863, General William Rosecrans of the Union army had captured Chattanooga with a 55,000-man army. The defeated Confederates, under General Bragg, retreated south into Georgia. Very soon, however, General Bragg had received reinforcements from Virginia, and when his army reached about 70,000, he'd marched back into Tennessee and attacked Rosecrans. And damned if his Southern boys hadn't whipped Rosecrans at the Battle of Chickamauga! It was a proud day for the entire South and they'd celebrated to beat the band out at Wildwood.

After their glorious victory, General Bragg's army had decided to dig in at Missionary Ridge and Lookout Mountain. It had seemed like a good tactic until word arrived that General Grant—newly promoted to the rank of supreme commander of the Union Army of the Cumberland—had arrived to bolster the Union forces still holding Chattanooga. And then, dammit, only a few weeks later, General Sherman and General Hooker had both arrived with thousands more Union reinforcements! Now, to the surprise of no one, the greatly superior forces of the Union army were attacking the

Confederates dug in on the mountains and ridges. What had started as a Confederate siege on Chattanooga appeared to be on the way to becoming a bloody rout.

Ruff glanced sideways at Mason, who had not said much of anything since they'd eaten and ridden away from Wild-wood with all but the last few Ballou mares. "Mason?"

He didn't hear Ruff, who raised his voice. "Mason!"

"Yeah?"

"What are we riding into?"

"I can't say for sure, other than it's war."

"I know that."

Captain Denton twisted around in his saddle and shot Ruff a hard look. "Let's keep it silent back there!"

Ruff *couldn't* keep it silent. Not after another mile and with the sound of the battle growing ever louder. The young stallion between his legs was prancing, throwing its head around and snorting with growing fear.

"Mason," Ruff whispered, "can't you tell Houston and me anything?"

"It's a war up ahead," Ruff heard his brother say. "And it's not going well for our side."

Ruff waited for Mason to elaborate, but he waited in vain. Mason was like a stranger in the grip of a trance. He rode stiffly, eyes vacant and almost dreamlike. He didn't appear vigilant at all, which Ruff found very disturbing.

"Mason, how can you tell?"

There was a long pause and then his brother said, "I can tell by the sound of the artillery. Most of it is coming from the Union army. And I can *smell* gun smoke blowing down off Missionary Ridge and Lookout Mountain."

Mason reached down and scratched the neck of his own Ballou horse before adding, "I smell death, too, Ruff."

"Stop it!" Houston hissed at his older brother. "What are you trying to do to Ruff?"

Ruff figured he didn't need any protector from the truth. "Mason is not *trying* to do anything to me. He's just telling what he knows."

Houston's jaw muscles ridged but he kept his mouth shut as they continued on. Ruff would have felt a whole lot safer riding through the forest than brazenly riding up this big road on the way to Chattanooga, but since no one else was complaining, he kept his thoughts to himself and concentrated on the mares that they were leading. There were twelve altogether, and every one of them was in foal although none would deliver until next spring.

Ruff's own mount was growing increasingly nervous. Both he and Houston were riding three-year-old stallions. They were green broke and quite a handful. Ruff's horse matched Houston's both in size and its sorrel coloring, but Ruff's stallion was more fractious. Ruff considered himself the finest horseman in Tennessee, a fact not even Houston and Dixie would have argued. Now, however, it was going to take all his skill and knowledge to keep his stallion and the Ballou mares under control as the sounds of war grew ever louder. But first, Ruff wanted to know what they were getting into. He'd never been to war. It didn't seem so unreasonable to ask for particulars.

"Will we just . . ."

"Just what?" Mason asked.

Ruff stammered, "Will we just ride into the battle?"

"Of course not. I'll volunteer to scout up ahead."

"Oh." Ruff frowned and glanced at Houston, who did not meet his eye. Ruff said, "Mason, one of us ought to ride up ahead with you. Our mounts are a lot fresher than yours."

"Don't even think about it," Mason said with an edge to his voice. "I promised Pa that you wouldn't do anything but watch out for his mares and your stallions."

"But . . ."

"I *promised*," Mason snapped impatiently. "I gave him my word, and so did Captain Denton. So let's not talk about it anymore."

Ruff clamped his jaw shut and rode on. Mason, as easygoing a man as there was in the whole family, just wasn't himself anymore. But then, judging from the haunted look in his eyes and that of the rest of this patrol, war changed all men and none for the better.

When the sound of rifle and pistol fire could be clearly heard, scattered between the booming artillery, Captain Denton led his small cavalry patrol off the road and into the trees.

"Patrol, dismount!" Denton barked. "Lieutenant!"

Ruff watched as his brother moved up to the captain and he heard Denton say, "I want you to take one of those fresh stallions your brothers are riding and go scout on up ahead. Find out what we are up against. If the the area is filled with Union soldiers, we'll have to find a way to flank them so that we can get up to Missionary Ridge with these horses."

"Yes, sir!"

Mason returned. "You heard the man," he said. "I need to borrow a fresh horse."

"Take mine," Houston said.

Ruff shook his head. "Mine is a shade faster."

"But not as steady," Houston wisely pointed out. "Ruff's stallion is about as likely to throw a man as carry him out of danger."

Without a word, Mason took Houston's reins and mounted.

There was nothing that Ruff could do but control his nervous young stallion and the excited mares. It made Ruff furious that only his brother had been ordered to go on ahead into sure danger. But rather than demand an explanation of the captain and risk embarrassing Mason, Ruff kept his silence.

"Don't take any chances," Houston solemnly advised.

Mason touched his heels to the flanks of Houston's Thoroughbred. "I'll be back," he said without meeting his brothers' eyes. "And it won't be long."

When Mason rode away, Ruff cussed silently to himself. The artillery fire seemed to be located just over the next ridge, and that was Mason's direction.

"I'll give him an hour," Ruff said to Houston. "If he isn't back by then, I'm going after him."

To Ruff's surprise, Houston said, "If Mason isn't back in *half* an hour, *I'll* take your horse and find him."

It was then that Ruff realized that Houston cared a lot about Mason, even though they'd fought like hell through their childhood. Houston wasn't a man that showed much emotion. About the closest thing he'd come to letting you know he approved of you was to drive his knuckles into your shoulder hard enough to knock you sideways but not hard enough to make you mad. In that way, he was pretty much like their father. Ruff had heard it said that Houston was known to show a lot more affection toward the ladies of Chattanooga.

Houston pulled out his pocket watch and consulted it every few minutes. It made Ruff even more anxious and of the opinion that he, and not Houston, would be the one to go searching for their brother. After all, his was the freshest and strongest mount now in the cavalry patrol. It would do the stallion good to be run long and hard. It would settle him down.

"All right," Houston said at last, "give me your horse and you take these. . . ."

Ruff did not hear the rest of the request for he swung into his saddle and, ignoring Houston's curses and shouts, raced off to follow Mason's trail. Ruff twisted around in the saddle and looked back after he'd gone a quarter mile but he could see no pursuit by his brother. Houston would be fit to be tied, of course, but he could not risk pursuit because it would mean the Ballou mares would have no one in the family to look after them.

The stallion was flying and since the footing was good and the trail straight and narrow, Ruff let the horse have its head and run for all it was worth. He leaned forward over the withers, where his weight would be most easily carried, and he kept his rifle in close to his body so that it would not be torn from his hands by branches or thickets.

All of Ruff's attention was focused on the stallion's ears and the way it ran. The ears were laid back flat, which told Ruff that the stallion was angry and determined to show its stuff. And what stuff it had! Between each stride the Thoroughbred seemed to float for an instant before another burst propelled them forward. Despite being only eighteen, Ruff had already ridden hundreds of his father's racehorses. He knew that this stallion would have been one of his father's fastest yet and now he vowed to tell Justin that piece of good news, if they survived.

They must have raced a good three miles and all the while Ruff was so intent that his stallion did not stumble or pull up lame that he burst into a huge clearing before he even realized that it was occupied by a camp of Union soldiers. For an instant, Ruff was numb with shock and so were the enemy. Their faces were a blur as he shot directly through their camp, hurtling several wounded soldiers who gazed up at the underside of a flying horse.

"Long live Jefferson Davis!" Ruff shouted as his stallion caught a tent string and ripped down a tent, almost causing them both to somersault through a picket line.

Ruff kept the flying stallion on its feet by savagely jerking its head up and using his long, muscular legs to drive the animal forward rather than downward. The stallion faltered only a second, which probably saved Ruff's life, because he heard the sound of a bullet pass his right ear.

As he and the stallion plunged back into the forest again, Ruff heard scattered rifle and pistol fire. He let out a wild rebel yell and drew his own pistol to fire two rounds. Then, he reined hard to the east and tried to decide exactly how he was going to find Mason.

The problem was solved a few minutes later by Mason himself, who came shooting out of the trees. "You goddamn fool!" Mason cried. "What kind of a stupid stunt do you think you were pulling back there!"

"Hell, I don't know," Ruff said, his boyish smile dissolving. "It wasn't exactly planned, you know."

"I don't know anything anymore!" Mason cried, as they both reined their horses in behind a heavy thicket of dogwood, "except that it's a miracle that you didn't get yourself blown to pieces just now. The fact is, you *have* been shot!"

"Where!"

"You lost a piece of your right ear!"

Ruff reached up to touch wetness. He pulled his finger away. It felt as though his entire earlobe were gone. "Damn!"

"It serves you right. Looks like a rat-bit piece of cheese," Mason said. "But it definitely will make an interesting conversation piece when you are with our Southern belles. Now, we'd better ride!"

"Where to?"

"Back to Captain Denton. There's a company of Union soldiers heading straight in their direction. If we don't reach them first, they won't stand a chance."

That was all that Ruff needed to hear. He reined his horse after Mason and they went charging through the trees, giving the Yankee camp a wide berth. It was a wild, perilous ride and, more than once, Ruff was almost knocked from his saddle by a low-hanging limb. They sailed over logs and crashed through brush so heavy that Ruff thought his rapidly tiring young stallion would surely get its legs tangled and fall.

Somehow, they did find Captain Denton and his patrol. When they burst in among their friends, Mason yelled, "Captain, there's a company of Yanks heading right for us. We've got to move!"

"How far are they?"

"Less than a mile."

"Cavalry or soldier?"

"Soldiers with artillery."

Denton shouted to his men to mount up. Houston spurred his horse forward. "Captain, I demand to know exactly what you propose to do."

"I don't give a damn *what* your demands are!" Denton snapped. "My responsibility is to my men."

"And mine is to my brothers and our Thoroughbreds!"

Denton's thin lips pulled back from his teeth. "Lieutenant Ballou, inform your brother that unless he cooperates right now I will order my men to shoot him!"

Ruff's jaw dropped and he started to raise his rifle because he knew that you *never* gave Houston that kind of an ultimatum. He would rather die than back down. At just that moment, however, they heard a Yankee bugle, and then bullets began to cut through the air thicker than blow flies on a dead deer.

"Retreat!" Denton shouted, reining his horse around and spurring wildly into the deepest part of the forest.

The soldiers only had to take one look at the Yankees charging them to put new life into their exhausted horses. A moment later, Ruff and Houston found themselves in the middle of the wild retreat. Glancing at the soldiers on either side of him, Ruff took what small comfort he could muster from the fact that he did not see any panic. The boy riding on his left was no older than himself, hawk-faced, dirty and unkempt, but he didn't look at all afraid. Several times, Ruff looked back but he could no longer see the Yankees, and finally Captain Denton pulled his horse to a standstill.

"Everyone dismount!" the captain shouted. "We'll stage an ambush!"

The soldiers did as they were ordered. Houston and Ruff took the Thoroughbreds farther back into the trees and tried to calm them.

"This is madness!" Houston groused. "There's far too many bluecoats for those boys to fight. Even if they do kill seven or eight in the first volley, they'll still be overrun."

"There's nothing we can do about that," Ruff said. "All I know is that I damn sure ain't leaving Mason behind."

"Me neither," Houston said. He tied the mares to a tree and handed over his reins. "I'm going back and help. You'll have to stay with the horses."

"But dammit, I . . ."

"You went after Mason after I told you I was going, remember? Now it's my turn."

The last thing in the world Ruff wanted to do was hold the horses while his two brothers were fighting for their lives. But Houston was right, it was his turn with the horses.

It wasn't five minutes later that the Yankees came storming into Denton's trap. One minute all Ruff heard was the pounding of hooves and the smashing of brush, the very next moment it sounded like every rifle and gun ever made was being fired at once. Overhead, Yankee bullets began to break branches and they fell on the Thoroughbreds, causing them to dance, snort, and roll their eyes in fear.

"Easy, easy," Ruff crooned over and over as he heard Reb shouts and the death cries of Yankee soldiers. There was so much gunfire and chaos that Ruff couldn't tell if the Confederate boys had managed to break the Yankee charge. He desperately wanted to draw his gun and prepare to make his own stand but it was all that he could do just to manage the stallions.

Ruff's uncertainty seemed to last a lifetime. He could tell that the fighting was very heavy and he knew damn good and well that a lot of men were dying on both sides, especially among the Yankees. It was all he could do not to let the horses go and plunge back through the forest to help his brothers. But he told himself over and over that he also had an important responsibility and he could not afford to let his own high state of anxiety affect the Thoroughbreds, who were sensitive and hot-blooded enough to react to their master's fear.

Ruff crooned the old jumbled mix of Cherokee nonsense words preferred by his father, the ones that made no good sense but which best calmed and reassured the horses. The words flowed softly like an incantation, and even though the bullets kept raining branches on them and a cloud of gun smoke filled their nostrils, the horses quieted.

"Ruff!"

He spun around to see Mason and Houston burst out of the thickets. One look at his older brothers told Ruff that things were going from bad to worse.

"You and Houston have to ride for reinforcements," Mason gasped. "We stopped their charge but there are too many!"

"Then why doesn't Captain Denton order a full retreat!" Ruff shouted.

"The horses . . . most of them are down," Houston explained. "And we're being flanked."

Involuntarily, Ruff's eyes swept the forest from side to side. "Flanked?" he managed to repeat.

"Yes!" Mason tore loose the picket line that linked the Thoroughbred mares together. "I'm taking these mares up closer to the line. If it becomes obvious that we can't hold back the Yanks, they'll be our only hope of escape."

Ruff spun to face Houston. "But Pa said . . ."

"He'd understand," Houston said. "He'd say it had to be done."

Mason dug a paper from his gray uniform. His fingers, Ruff noticed, were still steady. "You and Ruff have to reach General Bragg. We are a scouting patrol and this is our report. Bragg must have it! Do you understand! He *must* have this information we've gathered on the enemy's troop movements."

"Damn the information!" Houston cried. "You need reinforcements!"

Mason started to say something in anger but then his expression changed. "Yes," he said as calmly as if he were standing on the steps of the church after Sunday service. "Of course we do. And Bragg will send them back with you."

Houston blinked. Words seemed to desert him and he gave Mason the strangest look. A look that caused Ruff's throat to ache. Houston's voice trembled when he said, "Come with us, Mason. Please."

"I can't. I've got to have these mares ready. Those boys can ride 'em out of here bareback if we're overrun. If I left right now with you, they'd have no chance of escape."

Houston nodded. "All right. Just don't wait too long for us to come back with those reinforcements. Just . . . just get on these mares and get out of here! They're scared and rough because they haven't—"

"Go!" Mason pleaded, cutting him off. "We're almost out of time!"

Houston turned his face away and, in a voice that Ruff didn't even recognize, he said, "Let's ride for Missionary Ridge!"

Ruff stuck his hand out and Mason took it. "You take care," Ruff choked.

"Same to you." Mason grinned. "And don't go riding through any more Union camps."

"Not very damned likely."

Ruff swung into the saddle. He looked down at Mason holding the Ballou mares and then, before he said something foolish, he turned and went racing off after Houston.

There wasn't time for a good-bye. They had to find General Bragg and they had to get Captain Denton's patrol reinforcements.

FOUR

Darkness fell very quickly on Ruff and Houston, who were forced to slow their horses to a walk. Their plan was to reach Missionary Ridge, where they hoped to find General Bragg and his besieging Confederate army, which had dug into positions overlooking the Yankees down in Chattanooga.

"We'll be plenty lucky if we don't get shot by our own sentries," Houston groused as they picked their way through the dark forest.

Ruff was riding stirrup to stirrup with Houston. Except for the creaking saddle leather and the muffled sound of hoofbeats, the forest was silent. There was no screeching of the great horned owl or scurry of game in the deep thickets. Ruff found the dead stillness after the thunder of war to be unnerving. It was as if everything—men, birds, animals and even the earth itself—were holding its breath until silence was again cannon-shot to hell at bloody dawn.

Ruff thought he must be going a little crazy, but then Houston said, "Damned if this night isn't spooky! But just over that mountain yonder are two armies and we'd better pray that the Confederates are still holding Missionary Ridge."

"If they aren't, we're riding to our deaths for certain," Ruff said.

Houston twisted sideways in his saddle. "I keep thinking we may already be too late to save Mason."

"Don't talk that way," Ruff growled. "He's got those

mares and he can always ride back home."

"But he wouldn't," Houston said heavily.

Ruff stared at his brother. "Why not?"

"I know him better than you, Ruff. He'd never run as long as there was fighting. Not even to save our mares."

Ruff's anger dissipated in the darkness and he felt a hollowness in the pit of his stomach. Houston wasn't the kind who got down on things very easily. And besides that, he did know Mason better than anyone else except maybe their father. Ruff felt more depressed than ever as they approached the back side of Missionary Ridge. And when they began to snake their way up, Ruff's nostrils twitched because the gentle night breeze was poisoned with gun smoke and the sickening stench of death.

But then he heard something in the breeze that made him sit up straight in his saddle and listen very hard. "Houston, do you hear it!"

"I do."

"Is that singing?"

Houston reined his horse up. He listened intently, moonlight highlighting his most prominent features. Houston was said to be the handsomest of the Ballou brothers, but Ruff was already the tallest. There was no question he would never be as attractive to women as Houston, especially with his new "rat-bitten" ear.

"It *is* singing," Houston declared. "Why, it's our boys singing 'The Bonnie Blue Flag'!"

Ruff expelled a deep sigh of relief and echoed the words to one of the South's most patriotic and popular Civil War songs. It was always sung with great spirit by both the soldiers and the loved ones they'd left behind, and the words never failed to bring tears to a Southerner's eyes.

We are a band of brothers, and native to the soil,
Fighting for our liberty, with treasure, blood, and toil,

And when out rights were threaten'd, the cry rose near and
    far,

Hurrah for the Bonnie Blue Flag, that bears a single star!
Hurrah! Hurrah! For Southern rights, hurrah!
Hurrah! for the Bonnie Blue Flag that bears a single star!

As long as the Union was faithful to her trust,
Like friends and brethren kind we were and just;
But now when Northern treachery attempts our rights to
    mar,
We hoist on high the Bonnie Blue Flag that bears a sin-
    gle star!

Hurrah for the Bonnie Blue Flag, that bears a single star!
Hurrah! Hurrah! For Southern rights, hurrah!
Hurrah! for the Bonnie Blue Flag that bears a single star!

Then here's to our Confederacy, strong we are and brave,
Like patriots of old, we'll fight our heritage to save;
And rather than submit to shame, to die we would prefer,
So cheer for the Bonnie Blue Flag, that bears a single
    star!

Spirits soaring, Ruff and Houston pushed their animals
hard the last few miles and when they topped Missionary Ridge, they saw a thousand Union army campfires
stretching all the way from Lookout Mountain to distant
Chattanooga and on to Chickamauga Creek. For almost
a full minute, they sat transfixed on their weary stallions
and surveyed the immense scope of the Union encamp-
ments being serenaded by the defiant Confederate troops
from their fortified heights above the valley. Ruff's spirits
plummeted.

"Even if there are only twenty or thirty bluecoats to
a camp, it still adds up to tens of thousands of Union

soldiers," Houston said. "And look how few there are of our boys in comparison up on Missionary Ridge."

"Yeah," Ruff said, "but they're still singing."

Houston swallowed loudly, then sighed. "And I'm afraid that tomorrow at dawn, the only singing that will be done will be Confederate angels winging their way heaven bound."

"Come on," Ruff snapped, reining his horse away, "we need to find General Bragg and get those reinforcements."

"There won't be any," Houston called. "General Bragg is too badly outnumbered!"

Ruff pulled in his weary stallion and tried to beat down his own bitter disappointment. "Yeah, you're right," he heard himself say. "So why don't we go back to help Mason? We could be there by dawn."

"Have you forgotten the message he gave us to deliver?"

"Damn the message! There's no message in the world worth Mason's life."

"*He* thinks there is!"

Ruff slumped down in his saddle because Houston had put his finger on the heart of the matter. They'd promised Mason they'd deliver this damned message that still just might contain information that was critical to General Bragg. Perhaps it even said that Confederate reinforcements were rushing to the general's aid.

"All right, let's find him," Ruff said, pushing his stallion on toward the flickering firelights up on Missionary Ridge.

They were challenged by a pair of sleepy-eyed boys with rifles but no shoes or coats despite the chill of the predawn hour.

"We've a message from Captain Denton!" Houston called out. "We need safe protection to deliver it to General Bragg."

One of the boys, a ragged youth that could not have been more than sixteen, lowered his rifle. "You don't sound like no Yank so I guess you're on our side. But you're still gonna have to throw down those rifles and pistols."

"I don't think I want to do that," Houston said after a moment's consideration.

The boy glanced nervously at his companion, who wasn't much older than himself and was standing with all his weight on one leg because the other was wrapped in a dirty bandage. "What do you think, Paul?"

"Hell, tell 'em where the general is and let 'em go! Maybe they have *good* news fer us. Do you have good news fer us?"

"I don't know," Ruff said, feeling ashamed because he was fed, clothed, and well mounted, while these half-starved boys were dressed in tatters. "But maybe."

"Got any food in those saddlebags?" the first sentry asked hopefully.

"Yeah," Ruff said, reaching back and unfastening one of the saddlebags.

He pulled out a chunk of cheese and half a loaf of bread. To his embarrassment, the two famished sentries dropped their rifles and jumped forward. One grabbed the cheese, the other the bread, and they began stuffing food into their dirty faces, gulping and making strangling sounds that caused Ruff's stomach to lurch.

"Well," Houston asked when the boys had finished devouring the food, "are you going to take us to General Bragg's headquarters or not?"

"Them are mighty fine animals you're a-ridin'," one of the boys said. "Back in Virginia, I used to work for a rich man who raised those tall, handsome horses. They was called Thoroughbreds. Is that what they are, mister?"

"Yes," Houston said.

The sentry turned to his companion, who was still chewing the last morsels of bread. "Paul, if I had me a horse that big and fast enough to almost-by-God fly, I'd ride him all the way to Califor-ni-ay and spend the rest of my life pannin' gold."

"It's all gone by now," the other said. "I'd ride up to the Comstock Lode like everyone else that was smart enough to go West before this war broke out. Besides Virginia City I hear tell there's a mountain of pure gold called Sun Mountain. They say them Comstock women are so pretty they'll make you either half-blind or half-crazy."

The pair laughed, really laughed, until one put his arm around the other's shoulder and had to be held up. Watching and listening to them gave Ruff a queer feeling. He thought the pair were loony, turned simple by the war and the death they'd seen and would see again tomorrow.

"Come on," Houston said softly, "we can find the general's headquarters on our own."

They rode away from the sentries, who kept laughing and whooping hysterically. That was when Ruff realized the hair was standing up on the nape of his neck.

"My name is Major Albert," the officer said, escorting them into his tent. "Whatever message you have for General Bragg you can give to me and I'll see that he gets it at the first opportunity."

"I think he ought to see it now," Houston said, pulling the message out of his own pocket. "I believe it contains vital information on Union troop movements."

"Let me see it," Albert said, extending his hand.

He was short but trim and appeared to be in his late forties, probably a former successful banker or merchant. His tent was very neat like the man himself. Major Albert would have been handsome except for the huge dark bags under his eyes. That, and the fact that he had a nervous tick at the corner of his mouth.

"Gentlemen," Albert said, "I have very little time. Give me that message!"

Houston glanced at Ruff, who nodded. "All right," Houston said.

Albert tore the envelope open and unfolded the scribbled message beside a candle on his camp table. He smoothed the paper, then read it very slowly, his lips moving just slightly under a thin mustache.

"It's worthless," he sighed, straightening and rubbing those awful eyes. "It informs our general that troops under Generals Thomas and Hooker have formed what they are calling a 'cracker line,' connecting the Bridgeport supply depot to Brown's Ferry, by road and by river steamer. This allows the Union to deliver supplies directly into Chattanooga. We can *see* that much."

"Is that all?" Ruff asked, stung by the thinly masked contempt in Albert's voice.

"No, it's not. It also tells us that General Thomas has been ordered to begin the attack by taking the high ground below us, and then General Hooker is supposed to storm Lookout Mountain—which he did yesterday."

"We've already lost Lookout Mountain?" Houston asked, his expression sick with disbelief.

"That's right. And now Hooker is deploying his army to attack our right flank tomorrow morning at dawn."

"Can you hold this ridge?"

Albert turned away, his face haggard and filled with bitterness. "We're outnumbered six to one. What do you think, Mr. Ballou?"

"I think General Bragg ought to be moving his army off this ridge tonight."

"For what purpose?"

"To save his men, dammit! There's no way that we can win against those odds!"

"Winning," Albert said, "is no longer the objective."

Ruff could not believe his ears. "Then what the hell is the 'objective'? Losing good men for nothing?"

Albert turned on Ruff, who towered over him. "You are . . . how old?"

Momentarily thrown off balance by the question, Ruff stammered, "Eighteen, but what has that got to do with anything?"

"Eighteen is old enough to fight," Albert said. "God knows I've lost a lot of fine, strapping eighteen-year-olds and many much younger. We've got drummer boys that are fourteen years old and they are often the first to fall on the battlefields."

The major's calm, sad voice ripped the anger right out of Ruff. "I didn't mean to say that I thought you wanted men to die needlessly, Major. My brother and I just don't understand why you or General Bragg would pit our boys against such long odds."

"It's because our objective is now to inflict as heavy a toll on the Union army as possible. And even though we are bound to lose tomorrow, we do hold the high ground and we will kill a hell of a lot of Yanks. Who knows, we might even get lucky and hold out for a few days. Even that would be a victory of sorts. That's why we dig in and fight."

"Any chance that General Bragg will send reinforcements to help Captain Denton and our brother?" Ruff asked.

"No chance whatsoever," Albert said, taking a cigar from his coat pocket, cutting its tip off and then stuffing it in his mouth. "The only question is, would you like to remain and help us fight the enemy tomorrow morning?"

"Not me," Ruff said, suddenly very anxious to leave. "I'm riding back to help Mason and to save our mares."

"Me, too," Houston said. "Major Albert, I'm sorry. You've got to do what you have to do and so do we."

"Of course. Good luck."

Ruff shook the major's hand and so did his brother. Then, without any more words and with a sense of foreboding, he hurried outside and remounted his stallion. "What a waste!"

"You mean coming here with a worthless message?"

"That and losing so many good men on both sides of the field."

Houston's voice shook with passion. "I hope our boys kill them damned Yanks five to one!"

Ruff touched his heels to the flanks of his exhausted stallion and he led the way back through the Confederate lines. The singing had died out and very soon so too would the thousands of Union campfires below. Try as he might, Ruff could not muster any hatred for the individual Yankee soldier who waited out in that valley to throw himself into the teeth of death come the first light of day. Ruff came to realize that you couldn't hate an enemy because you thought it was your duty. No, if you hated an enemy, it was because you *felt* it down deep in your guts. Felt it like a knife twisting and turning so that the hate smothered every other feeling.

Ruff had never hated anything or anyone in his life. And no matter what happened next, he hoped he never would.

They heard the roar of Union artillery just after daybreak and then the rapid popping of rifle fire. The sound of battle intensified for the next quarter hour. Ruff felt sick at heart, guilty for not staying at Missionary Ridge and even angrier because he and Houston had not remained with Denton's patrol to fight.

"What if it's already over!" he cried out in anguish as they began to race their faltering stallions ahead. "What if Mason is dead!"

"If Mason is dead, then we'll take his body home and bury him."

Ruff blinked. He felt his chin dip in silent agreement. "Yeah," he said, "I guess that's what we'll do, all right."

When they grew near the place where they'd left Mason and the Ballou mares, Houston and Ruff dismounted, tied their horses, and readied their weapons. Without a word, they hurried forward, both filled with dread. And then suddenly, they were standing in a small clearing looking at a tangle of dead Confederate cavalrymen and horses.

"Oh, Jesus, no!" Houston choked.

Ruff lurched forward, his mind numb with the carnage. He tried to look straight ahead and avoid the terrible staring eyes of the Confederate boys whose faces were twisted and slashed, cast in a gray pall of death that matched their blood-crusted uniforms.

"Mason!"

The cry was torn involuntarily from his throat. Like a blind man, Ruff groped forward and then collapsed beside his brother. Mason was half-buried by the already-bloated carcass of a Thoroughbred mare. He had taken a saber slash at the base of his neck and his head was barely attached to his trunk. His face was crusted with black blood and his tongue was bitten off.

Ruff turned and vomited on an empty stomach across the flanks of another Ballou mare. In death, her brown eyes reflected terror, and Ruff saw that her beautiful sorrel coat was riddled from head to haunch. Her glazed eyes seemed to stare into the very core of Ruff's soul.

"Jesus!" he screamed, groping backward to touch Mason's stiff body. "Why! Why! Why!"

It took a long time before either he or Houston could look or speak to each other. And when they did, Ruff said, "We can't take Mason back this way. We can't let Pa and Dixie see what they done to him."

"He must be buried at Wildwood," Houston said. "We can find a blanket, or use our coats and wrap him up. Put him over one of our horses and . . ."

But Ruff wasn't listening. "You can do all that if you want. I'm going after them."

"Are you crazy? They'll kill you, too!"

Ruff felt his stomach start to heave again and he turned and staggered back into the forest, half running for his horse. When he reached it, he tore the reins free. The stallion rolled its eyes in fear and, had it not been completely exhausted, it would have bolted away in terror.

"Dammit!" Houston cried, grabbing Ruff by the shoulder and spinning him around. "I won't let you throw your life away!"

Ruff didn't recognize his own voice. "I don't think you can stop me except with a gun."

"Use your head!" Houston bellowed. "Think about Father and Dixie! There's nothing to keep the Union armies from marching all the way through the South now! Wildwood is next! We *must* be there to help!"

Ruff shuddered with the knowledge that getting himself killed was not going to bring Mason or the mares back. It would, however, be another stake driven into his father's heart. And yet, he could not abandon those poor Thoroughbreds to be broken or mutilated on some other battlefield.

"All right," he sighed, "but I'm going to find out if they took any of our mares. And if they did, I mean to get them back."

"But . . ."

"That's what I'm going to do!" Ruff shouted. "Now, you can bury Mason or take him back—that's *your* choice. I just made mine."

Houston clenched his fists at his sides and Ruff thought he was in for a fight. He and Houston had not really fought in years. And when they had, Houston had won because he was bigger and stronger. That wasn't necessarily the case now. They were both men. It would be a bad fight.

"All right," Houston said, forcing his hands to open. "We'll bury Mason in the woods by himself for now. Then, we'll go count our dead mares and see if any were taken. If they were, we'll try and get them back."

"No 'try' about it," Ruff said. "We *will* get them back."

"From the Union army?"

"That's right."

"How?"

Ruff didn't answer his brother because he had no answer. All he knew for sure was that there were plenty of dead Union soldiers around as well as Confederates. And though it would make his flesh crawl, Ruff figured he was about to wear the uniform of one of them dead, damn Yankees.

FIVE

"There are four missing mares," Ruff said, his haggard face appearing far older than his years. "All the rest were slaughtered."

Houston nodded grimly. He studied the piles of dead men and horses scattered about the forest clearing. "I wonder," he mused, "don't the Yankees even take the time to bury their *own* dead?"

"I don't know," Ruff replied. "Dead is dead, I guess."

"Let's get Mason out of here."

Ruff nodded. He followed Houston over to their brother's mutilated body. "How are we going to . . . ?"

"We'll pull a blanket from one of the dead saddle horses, then roll Mason up in it and carry him off a ways."

Ruff squatted on his heels. He was afraid he'd get sick again if he looked at what remained of Mason, so he let his eyes slip out of focus and tried hard not to think. That proved impossible. Ruff couldn't stop wondering if Mason had died quick . . . or slow. It was too hideous to imagine that Mason had lain wounded and helpless until his head had almost been severed from his body by a Yankee saber.

Ruff took a few deep breaths and ground the heels of his hands into his eyeballs. Hard.

"Here," Houston said, spreading a blanket out beside the body. "Let's roll him up and get this over with."

Ruff grabbed Mason's ankles and they lifted and carried him away from the stinking, bloated carrion of war. Mason

47

did not weigh nearly as much as he should have, and they took him a long, long way off until they entered a small patch of sunlit grass.

"We're going to need something to dig with," Ruff said. "I'll go back for a couple of sabers."

"No," Houston said. "I'll do it."

Ruff let his brother do the fetching. He sat down beside Mason's body, drew his knees up, and rested his chin as he listened for forest sounds. But there were none. The forest remained as hushed as the dead soldiers strewn about like so many fallen autumn leaves.

"We're going to get those mares," Ruff promised the corpse wrapped in a dirty horse blanket. "The way I see it, Mason, you died trying to save those mares and we are going to make sure that you didn't die for nothing. Don't matter what happens to us now. It's got to be done."

Ruff laid his big hand on the blanket. Mason was already stiff. "We'll be back for you after we get the mares. I promise that you'll be buried on Wildwood Farm. Getting the mares back and seeing you buried at home—that's all me or Houston can do for you now. That's just all we can do."

Houston returned shortly and they used sabers to cut and scoop out a shallow grave. They laid Mason to rest and then, to make sure that nothing feral disturbed his remains, they rolled and dragged a rotting log over the top of the grave.

"Let's find some Yankee uniforms and rescue those mares," Ruff said.

"We don't even know where to start looking."

"They can't be far. Maybe just a mile or two off. We can split up and—"

"No!" Houston lowered his voice and said, "Listen to me. I want to get those mares back as much as you do. But we are the only sons Pa has left now and I don't think he'd want to lose us over four horses."

Ruff managed a smile. "Four *Thoroughbred* mares with

Ballou bloodlines," he corrected, "and all in foal. That makes eight, and I believe he'd trade us both for that many. Yep. I'm sure he would."

Houston realized that his leg was being pulled a mite and some of the bitterness left his handsome face.

"Yeah," he admitted, "for eight Ballou Thoroughbreds I guess you're right."

That broke the deadly grimness of their mission and they both felt a little better as they swapped their civilian clothes for Yankee uniforms.

"I'm going to be a lieutenant," Houston said, stripping a dead Yankee officer. "Mainly because he wore my size."

Ruff had more difficulty. At a shade over six feet four, it took some doing to find a Yankee whose pant legs and sleeves were not ridiculously short. When he did find a tall corpse, the uniform was badly torn and crusted with blood. That made him hesitate.

"You can put it on," Houston said quietly, "or we can call this thing off and return to Wildwood."

Ruff gave a short, violent shake of his head and he yanked the uniform off the dead private and pulled it on himself. The dead man's scent assaulted Ruff's nostrils and made his flesh crawl.

"Let's mount up and find their tracks," Ruff grated hoarsely.

It took some doing to pick up the right set of tracks because the meadow was so violated by warfare. Ruff could see where the Confederate cavalry had launched an ambush. He could also see where the Union soldiers had charged across the clearing. The meadow grass was trampled and soiled with blood, churned up by the wheels of fast-moving wagons, for both artillery and ambulances. Circling the clearing were several trees that had been shattered by cannonballs—just splintered, fire-scorched stumps.

"Look," Ruff said, dismounting and looking eastward, "these are the marks of *our* horseshoes."

"No doubt about it," Houston said. "And they can't be

more than a few hours old. Do you see four sets?"

Ruff frowned. He was an excellent tracker, as were all his brothers. They'd hunted since early childhood and Justin had taught them how to read the sign of every wild critter in the Great Smoky Mountains.

"Here," Ruff said, kneeling down and closely examining another set of hoofprints.

"Well, that makes two of our missing mares," Houston said, not dismounting. "But what happened to the other pair?"

"I don't know," Ruff admitted. "Most likely their tracks were stamped out by wagon wheels, men, and the hooves of other horses. I expect that where we find two of our mares we'll find the other two."

"I expect so," Houston said. "Let's go."

Ruff mounted and rode after his brother. Now that they had agreed that they would not return to Wildwood without at least trying to recapture their father's Thoroughbred mares, Houston was very impatient. His plan was to overtake the Yankees and then wait until darkness to steal back the Ballou horses. If they were unfortunate to blunder across a Yankee patrol, their Yankee uniforms would give them enough of a surprise advantage to either escape or to sell their lives very dearly.

Either way, Ruff judged they were loaded for bear because, in addition to their own weapons, they'd found a few extra Army Colt pistols that the Yankees had missed before hurrying away from the battlefield. Coupled with the weaponry that they'd already been toting, they'd be able to fire nearly fifty shots before they'd have to reload. And while fifty shots did not mean fifty dead Yankees, it meant a lot of bluecoats would suddenly call on St. Peter.

They rode very cautiously all the rest of that morning. Quite often they came upon shallow graves in the forest where some poor Yankee soldier had been hurriedly laid to rest under a few inches of humus and a coat of dead leaves. The bodies would, of course, be eaten by animals but Ruff tried not to think of that.

In the middle of the afternoon, they heard the profane shouts of Union muleteers and hoarse cries of the Yankee wounded. A few minutes later, they heard two rifle shots and soon came upon a dead horse that had been ripped apart by an artillery shell and then not allowed to die until it had spent its last breath pulling some damned Yankee wagon.

"War is hard on soldiers but it's bloody hell on the livestock," Houston said darkly.

Ruff's stallion was so weary that all it could do was snort a little at the dead horse still wrapped in its leather harness. "At least they shot him clean in the head."

"Yeah," Houston said, "and that's more than they'll do for us if we're caught."

"I *won't* be taken alive," Ruff vowed. "I've heard about the Union prison camps. I'd rather die fighting."

"Me too," Houston said. "But I'd rather not die at all if I can help it."

There was a question that was eating at Ruff's mind and he let it out in the open. "What do you think happened back at Missionary Ridge?"

"All our boys are probably dead by now."

Ruff had the same awful suspicion. "If . . . if we hadn't tried to come and save Mason, would you have stayed?"

Houston gave the question careful thought. "I guess I would have," he said at last. "I don't believe I could have lived with myself had I walked away leaving our boys in such a fix."

He looked at Ruff. "What about you?"

"I'd have stayed," Ruff said. "Between us, we would have killed a dozen or so before they brought us down."

"We would have for sure," Houston said. "But I'm glad it didn't come to that."

"Me too." Ruff scrubbed his sleep-starved eyes. "In a way, Mason saved our lives. Have you thought about that?"

"I have and I wouldn't argue the point. If we'd have stayed with him we'd be dead and if we hadn't left Missionary Ridge last night to hurry back to help him this morning, we'd be dead again."

"A man can only die once."

"Not necessarily."

Ruff was about to ask his older brother exactly what the hell that was supposed to mean, but Houston suddenly threw his forefinger up to his lips as he reined up sharply.

Ruff listened and he heard the sound of leaves crunching under boots. He and Houston both bailed off their stallions and drew their Colt revolvers, listening to the crunch of leaves growing louder. Then Ruff saw the Yankee soldiers moving off about fifty yards through the trees. They were talking with a good deal of animation and paying no attention to their surroundings.

Houston holstered his pistol and drew his rifle from its scabbard. He raised it and took aim but only tracked the unwary soldiers until they disappeared. Then, he lowered the rifle and said, "Damn fools are probably from New York City or Boston or some such city. It's a wonder they're still alive, walking around in the woods that'a way."

"Well, if they were sent out as scouts or hunters, they sure are seven kinds of fools."

"Just as likely they're deserters," Houston said. "I hear tell that desertions are commonplace among Union soldiers."

"If they're winning this war, why'd they desert?"

"There are thousands of dead Yankee soldiers who—if they could speak—would tell you a man can win a war but still lose his life."

Ruff glanced up through the bare limbs of a maple tree. He judged it to be about four o'clock in the afternoon. "I'm thinking we ought to just ride into the Yankee camp and look for our horses."

Houston cocked an eyebrow. "Just like that?"

"Why not? If anyone gets suspicious, at least we've got a chance of escaping on these horses."

"I'm not so sure of that," Houston said, sounding dubious. "These young stallions will attract quite a bit of attention. And they're too worn down to outdistance fresh Yankee horses."

"I'm not *walking* into no Union army camp," Ruff vowed. "After all, we're horsemen. Not soldiers."

A faint grin lifted the corners of Houston's mouth. "You're right. We *are* horsemen."

With that decision made, they remounted and continued on, the Union army just up ahead.

When they came to the bank of a wide-flowing stream, the forest opened to reveal a large valley, and it was filled with tents, picket lines, artillery, wagons, and soldiers. All up and down the stream, men and animals were reposing, washing or collecting water for the evening camp.

"Whew!" Houston said, buttoning his officer's tunic and then letting his thirsty stallion drop its head to drink. "Are you sure we really want to ride into that lion's den?"

Ruff dipped his chin and tried to steady his nerves. "Lot of horses here. It could take a little time to find ours. Best we get started."

"Yeah, best we do," Houston said, waiting until their horses had slaked their thirst.

So they splashed across the muddy stream and rode into the Union camp not knowing or really even caring what companies they were passing through as they studied every picket line in search of their Thoroughbred mares.

No one paid them any attention. A few men gave the Ballou stallions a good, admiring look, but most were too tired or occupied to care. Ruff was astonished to see how many Yanks carried the wounds of war. It seemed a good half of them were limping or wearing an arm in a sling or had some other kind of battle wound. Here and there, he observed soldiers stretched out on blankets as their friends comforted them in their final, agonizing hours.

One man, whose lower jaw was missing, raised the upper part of his body when they rode past and stared at them wild-eyed. Ruff looked away quickly. He did not want to make eye contact with anyone and risk the chance of being drawn into a conversation where their Southern accents might arouse suspicion, though that was not likely, since many Southerners had turned traitor and decided to go north and fight for the Union.

"Say there!" a man called. "Lieutenant! Hold up a minute!"

Houston reined his horse to a standstill. He and Ruff both twisted around in their saddles to see another pair of lieutenants coming in their direction.

"Just keep riding," Houston hissed. "I'll stay and handle this."

"Good luck," Ruff said, nudging his mount forward, eyes restlessly moving up and down the Yankee picket lines.

He came upon a pair of soldiers who were opening sacks of grain for a string of good-looking horses.

"Say there," Ruff said, "you willing to sell me a few pounds of that grain?"

The soldiers looked appraisingly at him and then his stallion. One said, "This here grain is for these officers' horses. You ain't no officer."

"No, but this was a Confederate officer's horse before I shot him out of the saddle." Ruff jerked his thumb over his shoulder. "And Lieutenant Ballou back there, he's an officer and he'll want to buy a few pounds for this stallion's twin brother."

"Damned if they aren't a pair of fine-looking animals," one of the soldiers said, "but if we were to get caught selling this grain, we'd. . . ."

"Here," Ruff said, dragging one of the Army Colts from his waistband. "I'll give you this pistol, which you ought to be able to sell for a few dollars. As you can see, this horse is half-starved."

"He does look hard used," the soldier allowed. "But if

you caught him in a fight, he's gonna be taken by some officer. Privates like us don't ride blooded Thoroughbreds."

"Well," Ruff said, "you're probably right but that don't change the fact that this is too fine a horse to let starve."

The short, fair-haired soldier, smiling, nudged his friend and said, "What's a couple pounds of grain going to hurt, Ed?"

"Yeah," the taller one said. "And we can damn sure use some trading bait. Wages ain't too good for men of our rank, as you well know."

The two soldiers looked around to make sure no officers were paying them any notice, and then they hurried over and grabbed two small burlap sacks of grain.

Ruff handed over the pistol and laid the sacks across the front of his saddle. "Much obliged, boys. And by the way, I've heard that there are four or five Thoroughbreds to match these in camp. Probably came from the same horse ranch in this part of Tennessee. You happen to see them?"

The two exchanged glances. The shorter one said, "Seems to me I saw a pair of 'em late this afternoon. Could be most anywhere around the camp. Sorry I can't help you any more than that."

Ruff smiled. "You've been more help than you know."

"Damn fine animal," the taller one offered, "but I still say he'll catch the eye of some captain or major and you'll be afoot by tomorrow—mark my word."

"You're probably right," Ruff said, touching his heels to the stallion and riding off to rejoin Houston.

"Here," Ruff said, tossing his brother one of the sacks of grain. "Let's find a place by the stream and give these poor stallions a good feed and rest."

"I'd say we keep hunting for those mares while there's still some daylight," Houston argued.

"Nope," Ruff said, " 'cause I don't know about you, but I can feel this stallion starting to shake because he's so weak and played out. Unless they're fed and rested for a couple hours, they're not going to be much help if we got to leave on the quick."

"All right," Houston said, "but we still have to find those mares before dark."

"You feed and watch over the horses," Ruff said, "and if our mares are in this camp, I'll find them!"

"Nope. Bad plan."

Ruff frowned. "Why?"

"Wouldn't look right for a lieutenant to be standing around taking care of a private's horse, now would it?"

As much as it galled him, Ruff had to agree. "All right," he said, "then I'll stay with the horses and you can scout out the mares."

Houston was not a man who loved to walk any distance, but then none of the Ballous would walk ten feet if they could ride. Still, he seemed pleased as he brushed his lieutenant's uniform off and struck out across the valley. Ruff watched him disappear among the tents and then set about giving grain to the famished stallions.

"You boys are going to survive all this," he promised them. "But as for the easy life of the aristocracy that you've enjoyed to date, well, that will change if General Sherman or General Grant and his army come to pay us a visit at Wildwood."

Houston returned just as the sun was plummeting into the treetops. He'd found a cheroot and a bottle of rye, which Ruff judged he had sampled liberally.

"Did you find them?"

"I found two," Houston said, not bothering to offer his brother a cheroot or drink, "and I figure they won't be too hard to steal in a few hours."

"Only two?"

Houston walked over to his stallion, who was consuming withered meadow grass as if it were pure molasses. He scratched behind the stallion's ears and then took another drink, squinting one eye.

"Don't you dare get drunk on me," Ruff warned. "We got horses to steal and a brother to dig up and bring home for a burial."

"Yeah," Houston drawled, "I know that, and I won't get drunk until that is done. But I got some hard news that needs telling."

"Then tell it."

"I made friends with another officer. My money bought us both rye and cigars—and he knew where the two mares were picketed."

"That's not hard news."

Houston thumbed back his campaign hat and took another pull on his bottle. "The hard news is that Captain Denton—*our* Captain Denton—ran off from Mason with the other two mares."

"What!"

"That's what I was told. Him and some other officer took the mares and left Mason to die."

Ruff stepped forward and yanked the bottle out of Houston's fist. He raised and poured the fiery liquor down his gullet until his eyes bled tears and the rye was gone. He hurled the bottle into the stream and took a deep breath. "Any idea where Denton went?"

"No." Houston scowled. "He might have been heading for Missionary Ridge."

"Or he might have been running for his damned life!"

"Yeah," Houston said, "that too. Guess we'll never really know."

"Don't count on it."

Houston stepped up close to Ruff and his voice took on an edge. "I agreed to come with you and help you find our mares. Now, you've got to help me steal them and dig up Mason. We can't be worrying about Denton or any other damned thing. Is that understood?"

"It is."

Houston relaxed. He placed his hand on Ruff's shoulder. "I know what you're thinking about Denton. How you'd give anything to get your hands on his neck and wring the truth or the life out of him. But don't jump to conclusions against the man. Maybe he thought he had to reach General Bragg to tell him something. Maybe . . ."

Ruff shook his head. "I'm telling you, Denton ran to save his life."

"Take it easy," Houston said. "Someday, if we live through this war, we'll come across Captain Denton and those mares. When we do, we'll learn the truth."

"For Mason."

"For Mason," Houston repeated.

Ruff stepped back. He turned and walked heavily over to the stream. He collapsed on his knees and dunked his head in the cold, flowing water. It helped. But finding Denton would have helped a whole lot more.

It was just before midnight when they tightened their cinches and remounted. The stallion between Ruff's long legs felt like a different animal than the one he'd dismounted five or six hours before. It was still very tired but with grain, grass, water, and rest, it had regained a spring to its step and Ruff figured it would be able to run.

"Follow me," Houston said, leading off across the valley, then snaking his way into the big army camp.

It was almost ethereal, riding through the darkness, seeing the firelight lick at the faces of thousands of staring Yanks. Ruff kept his eyes focused between the ears of his stallion and let it follow his brother's horse for nearly half an hour until Houston reined up quite suddenly.

"The picket line is just ahead."

"How are we going to do this?"

"We'll try it the easy way first," Houston said. "I'll search out that lieutenant that was so accommodating this afternoon. Get him to order the sentry to let us have our mares."

"Why should he do that?"

"Beats the hell out of me," Houston said, dismounting

and handing his reins to Ruff. "But I can't think of any other way to go about doing this peaceably."

Ruff shook his head, wondering if his brother was drunk. Maybe the bottle of rye he'd seen was the second or the third instead of the first. Houston could hold his liquor better than most and you could never quite tell if he was drunk or sober. But since his brother had already disappeared into the Union camp and Ruff found himself holding two sets of reins, there was nothing to do but play this out to the end.

A full hour passed and Ruff's empty belly was tied up with worry before he saw the familiar silhouette of Houston emerge with his arm around another man.

"Private Ballou," Houston called, "bring those two Thoroughbred stallions forward on the double!"

Ruff scowled, not liking the officious tone of his brother's voice or the slur of his words. But he did as he was told.

"Lieutenant Wise, this is Private Ballou and the two stallions I was telling you about. Ain't they special!"

The Union officer took an unsteady step forward. "I can't see them, it's so dark." His voice was thin and carpish. "Why don't you have him bring them up to the campfire."

"Naw, they're too damn unruly. You know how us studs can be!" Houston jammed an elbow into the Union officer's ribs hard enough to cause the much smaller man to audibly grunt. He continued. "All we want you to do is tell them sentries on the picket line to let us have them two Thoroughbred mares to breed to these Thoroughbred stallions."

"But don't the mares have to be . . . well . . ."

"Well, what!"

"Well," Lieutenant Wise stammered, "you know . . . ready for it."

Houston erupted in raucous laughter. "They're females, aren't they! Females are *always* ready for it!"

"My wife is the exception to that rule," Wise lamented.

Houston laughed even louder but Ruff detected that the

laughter was forced and that told him that his brother was still reasonably sober and that this was all a charade.

"Aw, come on, Lieutenant! It'll only take a few minutes and you can even watch."

"I don't *want* to watch," Wise insisted. "And I don't understand why all this breeding business can't wait."

"Because of the moonlight!" Houston exclaimed. "That's when they have the best chance of getting with foal."

"It is?"

"Sure! Don't you know anything about horses?"

"No, I don't. I don't even like animals. And my wife never . . . well, I don't want to talk any more about this."

"Good!" Houston said, grabbing the man by the arm and hustling him off toward the picket line. "Neither do I! I'll take care of everything and when the breeding is over, we'll have those mares pregnant. Your superior officers will be delighted."

"I hope so," Wise whined, "but I think you're drunk as a loon and twice as crazy."

Houston guffawed, pounded Wise on the back hard enough to drive him forward, then disappeared. Ten minutes later, Ruff saw him come leading the two Thoroughbred mares out of the darkness.

"Let's ride!" Houston said, swinging into the saddle and handing a lead line to Ruff while he dallied the other lead line around his saddle horn.

Ruff didn't need any encouragement. He set off at a rapid trot that carried them into the trees and then out of the valley. Moving south, toward Wildwood Farm.

SIX

Dixie placed the tray of hot chicken soup beside Private Jim Wilson's bed.

"It smells delicious," he said, pushing himself up against the headboard.

"While it cools enough to eat, I'll change that bandage."

"You changed it just yesterday," Wilson complained.

"I know and I'll change it again tomorrow. If you get an infection you could die of blood poisoning."

The young Confederate frowned. He was of average size, though very thin, and his eyes were soft brown, the color of tanned buckskin, like his hair.

"How come a pretty girl like you wears a man's pants?" he asked as Dixie peeled off the bandage and inspected the thick scab. She poked hard at his shoulder.

"Ouch!"

"Hurts, huh?"

Wilson recoiled hard against his pillow. "You're darned right it does! And you don't need to poke and jab at me like I was a horse or a mule."

Dixie smiled sweetly. "If you were an animal, I'd be much more careful, Private. And you'd be a better patient."

Wilson blushed. "I swear that I don't know why you treat me so mean, Miss Ballou. I realize I'm a bother, but I didn't exactly get shot huntin' possum."

Dixie felt a stab of guilt. Of course he hadn't, and she should have been more gentle with this young soldier. But

61

the truth of the matter was, she felt uneasy about the way he looked at her. It wasn't like a friend and it wasn't in a brotherly way.

"How old are you, Miss Ballou?"

She slapped a hot compress on his shoulder and his eyes bugged with this sudden jolt of pain. "*Owwww!*"

"Too hot, huh?" Dixie said with a bright smile. "Sorry. Now, what was that impertinent question you asked me?"

"Never mind!"

"All right."

Avoiding the private's accusing eyes, Dixie applied a little horse liniment to speed the healing, and then finished redressing the wound.

"You ought to be on your feet and heading for your company in a few more days."

"There ain't no hurry. I don't guess I want to rush off and get myself shot again."

Dixie picked up Wilson's soup and shoved it at him, spilling some on his chest.

"Ouch! Dammit, Miss Ballou, now you're trying to scald me!"

"Oh, I am sorry," she said with mock concern.

"You're trying to drive me away before I get healed, aren't you? That's what you're trying to do. I got it figured out now. Well, it won't work!"

Dixie bristled. "Private Wilson," she said, "you can either go on your own accord or I can see that my father runs you off at the point of a gun. I would just think that the former would be more dignified."

"You're gonna be a pretty woman," Wilson said, mopping the soup from his chest, "but you'll be a heartbreaker. I'd have no part of you."

"Oh," Dixie mocked, "what a pity! Bye now!"

She left the room with a barely concealed smile and almost collided with her father.

"Dixie, are you tormenting that poor young soldier again today?"

"Why, no, sir!" she protested. "I was only bringing him some hot chicken soup."

"I heard him shouting. What did you do," Justin asked, "scald the poor fellow?"

"Well," Dixie said, struggling to keep a straight face, "I guess I *might* have spilled just a little hot soup on his chest."

Justin shook his head. "How such a sweet and gentle woman as your late mother could bear such a vixen as yourself is beyond me."

Dixie smiled and passed on by to the kitchen. Justin went inside to visit the young soldier.

"That daughter of yours has got a mean streak a mile wide!" Wilson exclaimed. "What's wrong with her?"

"Nothing that falling in love and growing up won't cure," Justin said, pulling up a chair beside the private's bedside. "How are you feeling?"

"Until your daughter came in here, I was feeling just fine."

"I'll see that the household servants bring your meals and change that dressing from now on."

The private scowled. "Aw," he said, "I guess I'd rather Miss Dixie did it. No offense, sir, but your daughter *is* kind of pretty."

"No offense taken," Justin said. "She bears quite a resemblance to her late Cherokee mother."

"She told me she was part Indian. Hard to believe."

"Why? A great many of the Cherokee are a tall, light-skinned people. And they are as educated and cultured as most whites—more so, in fact."

"Yes, sir, I didn't mean to . . ."

"Never mind," Justin said. "Where are you from, boy?"

"Mississippi. But I wound up with the Army of Tennessee."

"Then you've seen some hard fighting."

Wilson nodded. "Everyone from my hometown that signed up to fight is dead now, I reckon. Leastways, all that I know of."

"How did you come to get hooked up with Captain Denton?"

"He came through our camp asking for volunteers. Said he wanted only the finest horsemen for 'special patrols,' as he called 'em. Like anyone who could sit a horse well, I'd dreamed of riding with General J. E. B. Stuart and his raiders. But I never got the chance, so I volunteered to ride with Captain Denton. It beat serving in the infantry."

"I'm sure it did. Tell me, did Captain Denton lead you well?"

Wilson looked away. "If you don't mind, sir, I'd rather not answer that question."

"That's what I thought," Justin said as he rose from the chair. "At least tell me this much: is he a man of his word?"

"He is a Southerner, sir."

"That was *not* the question. Private Wilson, you know that my son, Lieutenant Mason Ballou, is with that patrol."

"Yes, sir, and your son is as fine an officer as I ever hope to have the honor of serving," Wilson said, "but he isn't in command—Captain Denton is."

"I know that," Justin said. "What do you know about General Bragg and that army he's got dug into Missionary Ridge and Lookout Mountain?"

"Not much sir, except . . ." Wilson swallowed noisily. "Except they're outnumbered six or seven to one. Don't matter how hard they fight. You can't beat those kinds of odds, can you now?"

"Not likely," Justin said, turning away to hide the worry in his face.

"Mr. Ballou?"

Justin turned. "Yes?"

"I mean no disrespect, sir, but how old is that daughter of yours?"

Justin suppressed a grin. "She's not interested in men or boys yet, Private. I'm afraid you had better leave Dixie to her horses."

"She's pretty high spirited, ain't she? Like your horses, I mean."

"She is for a fact. A little spirit is good in both, wouldn't you agree?"

"A little, I guess," Wilson said, not sounding very convincing, "but not too much."

"When will you be fit to ride again, Private?"

"Soon," the young man said. "But, sir, I got no horse now and . . . well I know there are none here to borrow. I had my own when I joined in Mississippi, but it was killed last summer."

"I think we can find you another mount," Justin said, "but it won't be one of my Thoroughbreds."

As Justin started to leave, Wilson called, "Sir, I'm not going back to fight anymore."

Justin turned and frowned. "What is that supposed to mean?"

"I'm going home," Wilson said defiantly. "I've lost my horse and this shoulder ain't never going to be the same."

"I see. Well, in that case, Jim, tomorrow morning you can climb out of that bed and walk the hell back to Mississippi," Justin growled as he turned and walked away.

The same afternoon, Ruff and Houston came riding their stallions up the road from Chattanooga leading the two recaptured mares. Across one of them was draped Mason's blanket-wrapped body.

One of the slaves saw them first and let out a whoop, then the others started calling, and pretty soon they were all coming to greet the two weary brothers. But when they saw the body, their smiles died and they fell back with fear in their eyes. Judging from the body's size, it was pretty obvious that another of the Ballou sons had come home to rest in peace.

Watching them, it occurred to Ruff that the Ballou slaves would have to be set free before the Union armies of Grant and Sherman arrived and that maybe this was not such a bad thing. The Ballous did not own a great many slaves and, unlike the cotton fields, where the work was hard and tedious, working with the horses was easy and unhurried. The slaves on Wildwood Farm were happy, and Ruff wondered if they would fare nearly as well on their own. He hoped so and supposed that the Union armies would feed and take care of them until the war was ended.

That this Civil War would and must end within the next few years seemed pretty obvious to Ruff. With General Bragg's almost certain defeat, only General Joe Hooker and General Robert E. Lee's armies remained a viable force against the North. And even they did not offer great hope, for the reports that reached Tennessee said that both Confederate armies were suffering from lack of supplies and food as well as ammunition and all the other necessities of war.

Ruff saw his kid sister and then his father emerge from the mansion to stand on the wide front veranda.

"This is going to be hard," Houston said. "Why don't you let me do the telling."

"Suits me fine," Ruff said, "but I don't think you need to tell about the saber slash that Mason took across the neck."

"I won't. I'll tell Pa that Mason was shot in the head and died instantly."

"Good."

When they drew up before the mansion, Dixie said in a small voice, "It's him, isn't it. It's Mason."

"Yeah," Houston said, eyes reaching out to his father. "I'm sorry, Pa. We were trying to deliver a message to General Bragg when it happened."

Justin slumped a little. He grabbed the porch rail for support and steadied himself. "And the other mares?"

"Two are missing. We heard Captain Denton and another officer took them and ran off. The others . . . well they're gone, Pa. We're sorry."

The old man nodded. He started down the stairs toward his son's body but Houston jumped off his horse and blocked his path. "Pa, I don't think you want to see him."

"Step aside!"

Houston stepped aside. His face looked stricken as Justin walked over to the blanketed corpse and reached out to touch the still figure. The mare shifted nervously, eyes rolling like marbles in a glass jar.

"Take him over to where his mother lies," Justin said. "And let's get him buried before sundown."

Ruff took up the mare's lead rope and led her across the yard to where his mother was buried. Ignoring the stench of death, he eased Mason down and Houston brought two shovels. Wordlessly, they started to dig.

Just before sundown they read passages from the Bible and then finished the burial. Through it all, Dixie stood by quietly but with tears streaming down her cheeks. Justin's craggy face was impassive, like dried parchment stretched thin and very brittle. When he read from the Bible, his voice sounded ageless, and when he turned and went silently back to the house, he looked bent and very old.

"What now?" Ruff asked his brother.

"I don't know about you," Houston said, "but I'm going to get a bottle and get quietly drunk."

"That won't help," Dixie said, breaking a long silence.

"Well," Houston said, "it damn sure won't hurt none, either."

The next morning, Jim Wilson climbed out of his bed, stretched his legs, and headed up the road for Chattanooga after saying a very quick good-bye.

"Son, you won't come across Mississippi in that direction," Justin called.

"I know."

"You going to let him walk away like that?" Dixie asked of her father.

"I am," Justin replied. "But that don't mean that you couldn't pack him some food for the road. Might be he won't find anything to eat for days—if he lives that long."

Dixie whirled and ran back into the house. A few minutes later, she came flying out the door with a pillowcase stuffed with bread, cheese, and even a smoked ham. She bounded off the veranda, raced to the barn, and came galloping out on the bare back of one of the mares.

"Look at her ride," Justin said to his sons with a pride. "If she was a man, she'd put even you to shame, Ruff."

"On the back of a horse," Ruff said, "she surely holds her own with any man."

Dixie and the mare went galloping up the road, and when Dixie came upon Private Jim Wilson, she drew her mare up and hopped down.

"What are you doing riding like that!" he asked.

Now that she had overtaken the soldier, she felt embarrassed. "Well, I . . . my father thought you ought to have some food for the road. And you forgot it so I brought it for you."

She shoved the pillowcase at him.

Wilson grinned broadly. He opened the pillowcase and peeked inside. "Why, lordy, Miss Ballou, this is more food than a Johnny Reb needs to march and fight on for six months!"

Dixie beamed. "I hope you live through this war and get home alive, Mr. Wilson."

He looked up from the pillowcase. "Do you, Miss Ballou?"

"Yes."

"And here all the time I thought you didn't like me."

"I like you, all right. I just like horses better."

Wilson clucked his tongue. "Damn, but I wish you were just a year or two older. Maybe you'd feel a whole lot different."

"About what?"

"Me and horses."

"I'll *always* love horses most."

The private's grin faded. "Well, that would be a real

shame if it comes to pass. A real honest-to-goodness shame."

Before Dixie could argue the point or get back on the mare, the soldier dropped his pillowcase and kissed her mouth—hard.

"Yeck!" she cried, fighting and clawing to get free.

Wilson released her. He looked at her with astonishment. "Didn't that make you feel *anything*?"

"It made me want to throw up, damn you, Jim Wilson! What did you want to do a fool thing like that for!"

He picked up his pillowcase of food and sadly wagged his head. "Never mind. But I'm *not* sorry I kissed you. Good-bye, Miss Ballou. And God help you when the Union army comes up this road."

With that, he turned and continued on up the dusty road. Dixie wiped her lips hard with the back of her sleeve and made a horrid face. She called, "Horses kiss better than you, Jim Wilson! You hear me?"

In answer, she heard his receding laughter filter back through the forest as he continued up the road toward Chattanooga.

SEVEN

After dinner, Justin Ballou invited Dixie and his sons into his library. He poured everyone a brandy and eased down in his favorite leather chair.

"It is time that we made a hard decision," he told them. "And I think you can guess what I am talking about."

"You're talking about what's going to happen to Wildwood Farm," Dixie said when her brothers remained silent.

"Yes," Justin said, "and what will happen to us and the last of our horses."

The old patriarch looked to his two tall sons. "You are the ones that will have to save our foundation breeding stock. You know how many years it has taken me to develop the bloodline."

"Thirty years," Houston said.

"Thirty-one," Justin corrected. "In a card game in Richmond, Virginia, I won my first Thoroughbred stallion not six months after he was brought over from London, England. He was wild and unruly—an outlaw, really—but I tamed and gentled him to race. It took me just three years of running him to buy this farm and a handful of the best Thoroughbred mares in America."

The Ballou sons and daughter listened intently although they had heard this story many, many times. That first stallion's name had been High Dancer and it was from his loins that all the generations of Ballou Thoroughbreds had sprung. High Dancer had died before Dixie was even born, but there was a huge picture in this library encircled by a gilded frame even more impressive than those found in the capitol building.

Justin surveyed his own offspring. He nodded with approval. "High Dancer is gone but his lineage is strong. High Man is every bit as fine a horse as his father, and those two young stallions you boys are training promise to be winners."

Justin exhaled a cloud of smoke. "The question is, how are we going to save our studs and the last of our mares from being lost to this miserable war?"

Ruff looked to his older brother, thinking to give him first crack at a reply. But when Houston and even Dixie remained silent, he said, "The Northern armies will be coming right through here. My guess is that they'll be marching to take Atlanta next."

"You have any facts to back that?"

"No," Ruff admitted, "but it makes sense. Atlanta would be my next target if I were General Grant. It's the key."

"I think you're right," Justin said.

"Pa," Houston said, "if they're coming, we have to get out of here in a hurry. There is no choice. Those damned Yankees will sack this house. They'll burn down the barns and fences, take everything of value, and—if we are very lucky—leave us with nothing but our lives."

"So we run?"

"Yes," Houston said to his father, "we take what we can save and go. We can return when the area is clear of Yankees."

"What do you think of that idea, Ruff?"

"It makes sense to me," he replied. "If we have a day or two, we can load wagons with the things most important to us. If we get out with the foundation stock, everything else can eventually be replaced."

"Dixie?"

She clasped her hands in her lap. "I hate the idea of running—even from an army," she whispered. "But I hate even more the thought of our horses dying in battle like those mares that we gave to Captain Denton. I just . . . just can't stand the thought of those poor things being terrified with cannonballs and bullets flying around them, driving them half-crazy."

"Then you must agree with your brothers."

She dipped her chin and her voice shook with fury. "To think of losing this beautiful home to the Yankees just makes me want to scream! I hate them, Father!"

Justin pushed heavily to his feet and came to stand beside his only daughter. "Don't hate them, girl. Hate will poison you."

"But . . ."

"I remember asking your mother about how she could live without hate after what the whites had done to her Indian people. Do you know what she told me?"

"No."

"She said that all hatred really came from love, it was just that the love had become twisted. She said that the more we hated, the more it meant we had been hurt, and the more we had been hurt, the more that we had loved. Do you understand that?"

"No."

"Sometimes I'm not sure that I do, either," Justin admitted a little sheepishly. "But I *believe* it and I believe your mother was one of the wisest women that ever lived."

"I'll try not to hate them so much."

"Good. And when we leave this place, we are going to take you over to your Aunt Maybelle's to stay for a while."

"Pa, no!" Dixie looked up with stricken eyes. "She's never even *liked* me."

"Oh, that is not true," Justin said, running his hand down his daughter's raven black hair. "She has begged me to take you since your mother died. She can make a lady out of you, Dixie. A real Southern belle."

"I don't want to be a lady!"

Justin shook his head. "Your mother wanted you to be raised like a lady."

"You don't know that!"

"Oh yes, I do," Justin said. "And I've failed on that account. Now, it seems to me, out of all the tragedy this war is bringing our way, at least something good will come out of it if you are schooled by your Aunt Maybelle."

Dixie came to her feet. "I won't do it!"

Justin's hand flashed and when it struck Dixie against the side of the face, she staggered. Dixie did not make a sound but paled, and tears filled her eyes.

"Pa," Ruff pleaded, desperately wanting to intervene. In all the years he could remember, Dixie had never suffered the sting of a hand or razor strop like the boys. Maybe that accounted for her being a little spoiled and so damned independent, but you couldn't start changing the rules now.

"Pa, she's never going to be like Aunt Maybelle. Not in a hundred years."

Justin turned away but they all heard him whisper, "I'm sorry, Dixie. It was wrong to lose my temper."

Dixie rushed forward and wrapped her arms around her father's waist and she cried.

Houston soon poured them all another stiff round of brandy and said, "Why don't we start out by agreeing that we have to take the horses and get out of here fast. In a few weeks, maybe months, we can come back and rebuild."

"The slaves will have to be given their freedom," Justin said to no one in particular. "I don't mind that. I doubt that any of them will be happy about leaving. I'll give them enough money for a start."

"Confederate money will be worthless," Ruff said. "Maybe you could let them take the household furnishings that they could sell or barter. Better they have it than the Yanks."

"You're right," Justin said. "That's what we will do. Now, the question is, where will we go?"

Again, because no one seemed to have any opinions, Ruff said, "Why don't we go over to the Oklahoma Indian

Territory and live among the Cherokee? I've always wanted to get to know Mother's people better."

"That's not a bad idea," Justin said, looking pleased. "They would help us. And maybe we could help them if the Union soldiers come and try to take their lands."

"I'd fight for them," Houston vowed. "I'm damned sick and tired of running from the Yanks. In fact, I'd about as soon make my stand right here at Wildwood."

"No," Justin said sharply. "There's a time and a place to fight. Like Shiloh and Gettysburg. But not here and not now. I won't lose the last of my sons for nothing!"

Ruff and Houston exchanged glances and dipped their chins in agreement. "So," Ruff said, "do we all head for the Indian Territory?"

"Dixie stays," Justin said. "It won't be for very long."

Dixie whirled and ran from the library. They could hear her shouting and crying all the way up the stairs to her bedroom.

"She'll get over it," Justin said. "Besides, a little culture will be good for her."

"She'll be miserable without her horses," Ruff said. "You know that as well as I do."

Justin's cheeks colored with anger. "Miserable? Well, I'm sick at heart at losing another son to this war! And the idea of handing over this farm to be pillaged and burned is almost more than I can bear! I'm even going to see that there is no trace of our family's graves so that some damned Yankee soldier doesn't take a mind to piss on their headstones!"

"They would do that?" Ruff asked with disbelief.

"Damn right they would!"

Ruff tossed down his brandy. "I'm going to bed. Tomorrow will be a long, long day."

"We had better send a few slaves up the road to watch in case the Yankees are already on their way."

Justin agreed. "Right. But from now on, we *ask* the Negroes to help us. Tomorrow morning, I'll tell them that they are free to come or go as they choose, and we'll work out something in terms of how they'll share what we leave behind."

Dixie was the first one up the next morning and she fed the horses long before dawn. She felt betrayed by her father, yet also sympathetic. Justin was doing what he thought was best, even though it was wrong and totally unfair. After the horses were fed, she gave them fresh water and brushed them until she was called to breakfast. Ignoring the call, she kept on working, her brush flashing until the sleek coats of these last Ballou mares were shining.

"You can't keep brushing them that way or they'll go bald," Ruff said, coming up behind her. "Why don't you come and eat?"

"I'm not hungry."

Ruff stepped over to the side of the stall and watched as Dixie worked the brush with a vengeance. "Pa is only doing what he believes is best."

She stopped brushing. "Oh, yeah? Well, what if he sent *you* to Aunt Maybelle's plantation so that she could bore you day and night by lecturing you on how to be a Southern gentleman?"

"She knows better than that. It'd never take. She gave up on me years ago."

"Well," Dixie swore, "she needs to give up on me, too!"

"She will, when you're a little older," Ruff said, trying hard to be the conciliator. "But it's different, you being a girl."

"I *hate* being a girl!"

"Since you act and dress like a boy, what's to be hated?"

Dixie brushed so hard that the mare grunted with pain and tried to step away. Dixie eased up. She looked at Ruff and said, "Can you keep a secret?"

"Sure."

"Promise?"

"I promise!"

"That damned Private Wilson kissed me! He kissed me on the mouth!" Dixie's face screwed up in a terrible grimace and Ruff started laughing.

"Don't you dare laugh at me!" she cried, raising the brush as if to throw it at him.

Ruff covered his head. It took him a moment, but he finally managed to stop laughing. "I'm sorry," he said sheepishly, "but it was the way that you said it. It sounded as if you had been kissed by a pig or a cow."

"It was almost that bad!" Dixie looked at her favorite brother. "Ruff, do you kiss girls that way?"

Ruff blushed deeply.

"You must or you wouldn't turn so red," Dixie said, resuming her brushing.

"Houston is the one to ask questions like that," Ruff blurted. "He's the expert on women."

"Houston fancies himself the expert on everything."

Ruff stuck his hands deep in his pockets. He wanted to mend some fences but he wasn't sure that he could. "Listen, Houston is your brother, the only one left besides me. And like Pa, he loves you."

"He thinks he knows everything."

"Well, he's smart. If you listened to him a little more instead of trying to argue all the time, you'd know that."

"You're a better horseman than he is."

"Maybe," Ruff admitted, "but there are lots of things he knows about horses that I don't."

"Such as?"

Ruff couldn't think of anything offhand. "You've got to help us," he said lamely. "We won't leave you at Aunt Maybelle's very long. I swear to it."

"How long?"

"A month. No more."

Dixie stopped brushing. "And you promise you'll come and get me in one month?"

"Well, now, I can't exactly put a time on it," Ruff hedged, "but—"

"One month!" Dixie cried. "If you don't come and rescue me from Aunt Maybelle after a month, I'll run away to the Indian Territory and find you."

"Now, dammit, Dixie, that'd be a foolish thing to do!"

She stood up. Tall for her age and willowy, lithe, and pretty, Dixie was going to be a looker, even though she possessed the temperament of a Missouri mule.

"I'll tell you this right now," Dixie said, "I'll give you 'men' one month and then I'm running away. And if I don't find you among the Cherokees, then I'll . . . I'll go to California."

Ruff rolled his eyes up into his head with exasperation. He headed for the barn door. "When you get like this, there's no talking horse sense to you, Dixie. No sense talking at all."

"One month!" she shrieked.

EIGHT

That morning was one Ruff figured he would rather forget. His father had called their slaves up to the house and explained that the Union army was marching south from Chattanooga and would soon be sacking and burning Wildwood Farm. The Negroes took this news quietly and most were concerned about what would happen to them next, though some of the younger men became excited.

Justin then told them he had signed papers granting each their freedom. Old Marilee, their dear housekeeper, had wept when she was told that the Ballou family would be leaving the freed slaves all the furniture except for that which had sentimental value.

"What about de chickens, de cats, and de dogs, Massa Ballou?" a young boy of about seven years asked.

Justin had chuckled and said, "Anything you can catch is yours, young man. All we are taking are the blooded horses. You people can keep the milk cows but we'll need the mules to pull our wagon. I know that you'll treat our animals well."

After that announcement, there wasn't much more to say. Justin would let Marilee decide how the furniture and household goods would be divided among her people.

By late afternoon, they loaded Lucinda's beloved piano and a few other pieces of furniture into the wagon, along with grain for the Thoroughbreds, their own personal belongings, and a mountain of horse equipment that had accumulated over many years.

"We'll spend one last night in comfort," Justin decided wearily. "It'll be better to leave at dawn."

Ruff, Houston, and Dixie thought that was a pretty good idea. They were all depressed and exhausted. The Ballou horses were nervous, sensing that all was not well, and the two young stallions were banging around in their stalls.

"The only thing on this place that looks happy and unconcerned is High Man," Houston observed.

Ruff mopped sweat from his brow and gazed off toward the paddock where High Man was standing, head up, ears pointed toward the road to Chattanooga.

Ruff did a double take and stared at High Man. "That old boy senses something coming our way."

"Maybe it's the boys Pa sent to give us warning," Houston offered.

"Can't be."

"Why not?"

"Because we forgot to send any," Ruff said. "Pa! Dixie! Grab your weapons! Someone is coming!"

Their ex-slaves scattered in fright as Ruff and Houston charged into the house to grab their rifles, pistols, and gun belts. They were back outside in just a few moments and this time they remained on the veranda, ready to fight.

"It's a Reb patrol!" Dixie cried. "Don't shoot 'em!"

Ruff lowered his rifle and looked sideways at his father, who also lowered his weapon.

Justin squinted into the dying sun. "Unless my old eyes are failing me," he growled, "it's Captain Denton, and he's riding *my mare!*"

Ruff blinked with astonishment. "You're right. It's the devil himself with a new patrol."

"I count six of them altogether," Dixie said.

"I want first shot at him," Houston announced, setting his rifle down and checking his pistol. "I want to be the one that puts a bullet through his cowardly heart."

"Hold on," Justin ordered. "We don't know exactly what happened when Mason died. And until we do for sure, there'll be no killing—at least not of anyone that wears a Confederate uniform."

"I wore the uniform of a Union officer," Houston growled, "and they'd sure as hell have killed me when I went into their camp to steal our mares back."

"That's different," Justin snapped, adjusting his old pepperbox pistol to a more comfortable position in his waistband. "So just hold up and let's hear what the man has to say—before I shoot him off my mare."

"I'll give Denton this much," Houston said quietly, "he's got plenty of nerve."

"His men look like they've ridden through hell," Ruff said.

Captain Denton slowed the Ballou mare to a walk as he turned off the road and angled slowly up the long gravel drive that led to the Ballou mansion. Beside him on the other missing Thoroughbred was a ferret-faced lieutenant who wore buckskin breeches in addition to his officer's tunic. There was a very bright red bandanna wrapped around his forehead. He wore moccasins instead of regulation army boots. Ruff had never seen such a scruffy officer.

"Isn't he a gem, though," Houston said. "But take a look at that rifle he's got lying across his saddle!"

"What is it?"

Houston pursed his lips. "I do believe the lieutenant has one of those new seven-shot Spencer rifles. I've heard tell that a Yank can load them on Sunday and shoot 'em the whole next week."

"If there's trouble, I'd say we had best drop him first," Justin said to his boys. "Dixie, go inside. You can shoot through the front window if there's a fight."

For once, Dixie didn't argue.

"Evening, Mr. Ballou," Captain Denton said, stopping in front of the veranda and raising his left hand in greeting. "Going to be a fine sunset coming upon us in a few minutes."

Justin nodded. "I am glad that you decided to return our Thoroughbred mares, Captain."

Denton thumbed his campaign hat back with his left hand. Ruff noticed that the captain's right hand did not stray far from the pistol strapped to his side. "Mr. Ballou, where's that pretty young daughter of yours? Out in the barn with her horses?"

"She's inside, probably fixing supper."

"I doubt that very much," Denton said, his eyes jumping from side to side before again settling on Justin. "Mr. Ballou, I regret to inform you that your fine son died in battle. However, we were able to give Mason a proper field burial."

"Is that a fact?" Justin shot back in a gravelly voice.

"It is." Denton turned slightly toward the ferret. "This is Lieutenant Clemson Pike."

"He's sorta out of uniform, isn't he?" Houston drawled, eyes never leaving the man with the new Spencer rifle. "He looks more like a turncoat than a Confederate officer."

Pike's eyes slitted. "And you, sir," he drawled with an Arkansas accent as thick and cutting as the Arkansas Toothpick sheathed at his belt, "look like a man scared to fight in *any* uniform."

Houston stiffened and might have gone for his six-gun if Ruff had not bumped his arm in warning.

Captain Denton said, "We have been in another hard fight. It matters very little if a man is in or out of uniform in times like these. All I care about is whether he can fight and obey my orders."

"What do you want?" Justin challenged.

"Hospitality—and more horses. My men and our mounts are hungry and tired. You have food, hay, and grain. I expect you also have a few empty bedrooms. Speaking of which, I want Private Wilson."

"He's gone."

"Where?"

"Damned if I know," Justin said. "Last time we saw him, he was walking up the road toward Chattanooga. Heading for the battle lines, I'd guess."

Denton's lips twisted with contempt. "Only until he was out of your sight, Mr. Ballou. After that, he'd be running for Mississippi. He's a deserter that will be reported and one day get his due."

"He was shot pretty bad, and he'll never have the complete use of that shoulder again."

"If I have my way, he'll be shot again," Denton said. "By a Confederate firing squad. Now, what about food and lodging?"

"Not for you or your men, Captain," Justin said. "Rein those horses around and ride back up the road."

Denton's eyes squinted. "Is that any repayment for the risks we took to bury your fallen son? Lieutenant Ballou died fighting next to me and—"

"You're a goddamn liar," Houston said in a soft, deadly voice. "Ruff and I found Mason's body and learned that you took our Thoroughbred mares and deserted the fight like a scared dog."

Denton turned ashen. He glanced sideways at his new lieutenant, who whispered something to the cavalry patrol. The four cavalrymen fanned out to flank their officers and their hands went to their pistols.

"I'm going to forget that you just spoke," Denton grated. "I'm going to forget how you just insulted an officer of the Confederacy while your *daddy* bought you out of this war."

"Is that right?" Houston said with a chilling smile.

Ruff's hand fingered the walnut grip of his Army Colt. Captain Denton might not realize it yet, but he was already a dead man. He'd crossed the line and there would be no turning back now. Ruff knew his brother, and he knew by the tone of Houston's voice that he was going to do his damnedest to shoot the captain out of his saddle.

"Mr. Ballou," Denton said, "as you can see, these men are hardened fighters and if you or your sons should do *anything* foolish, you will be shot down and remembered throughout the South as Northern sympathizers and as traitors."

Justin said nothing. Assuming that he had cowed the old man, Denton grinned coldly. "I don't think we need to act this way. We both know that the South deserves every ounce of our loyalty and sacrifice. And we *have* sacrificed greatly. All I want is that big stallion we rode by in the paddock and the rest of your horses."

Captain Denton shrugged his narrow shoulders inoffensively. "Mr. Ballou, I'll even let you keep one mare."

"How generous," Ruff said dryly.

"Now," Denton said, his voice taking on a steely edge, "what's it going to be?"

Justin found his voice, if you could call it that. When he spoke, it was to the four cavalrymen. "You boys had better rein those horses around and ride like hell while you can because the shooting is about to start."

Lieutenant Pike tensed and shifted the Spencer rifle so that the barrel was pointed toward the veranda. He said, "Be a terrible thing, a fine, prosperous Southern family like the famous Ballous to open fire on a Confederate patrol."

"The Confederacy is lost," Justin said. "This is between Captain Denton and me."

"You might think that," the ferret said, "but you and I both know that your family would be accused of treason. They'd be hunted down one by one and shot like rabid dogs. I hear you got a pretty little daughter, she'd be—"

Justin roared something and his hand jabbed at his waistband for the pepperbox. The lieutenant shifted the Spencer exactly a quarter inch and pulled the trigger. Justin took a slug in the chest and was knocked into Houston, who staggered, his own draw ruined.

Ruff alone stood poised and unimpeded as his hand streaked for his Colt. It came up fast and his first bullet ripped across the lieutenant's throat. Pike screamed, dropped his new Spencer, and clutched at his neck, blood spurting through his fingers.

Ruff shifted his aim and fired at Captain Denton, who simultaneously returned his blast. Ruff twisted around completely as he felt the impact of a bullet, and he struck the front wall with his face. He heard glass shatter as Dixie opened fire, and then he heard Houston's shouts, telling him to drop.

Ruff dropped to the veranda. The porch railing exploded with flying splinters as the cavalrymen opened fire. Ruff saw Captain Denton bent over almost double in his saddle as he wheeled the Thoroughbred mare around and tried to escape.

Houston forgot everything else and drilled Denton through the back twice before the captain pitched from his saddle and crashed to earth. Lieutenant Pike was also fleeing for his life. He was bent over and clinging to the neck of his Thoroughbred mare. Ruff fired at him but his shot went high because he was afraid of hitting the mare. He turned to see that Dixie and Houston had already taken a deadly toll on the cavalrymen. Two were dead and the other pair were spurring wildly up the road after their wounded lieutenant.

"Pa!" Dixie screamed, jumping outside with an empty gun clutched in her fist. "Pa!"

Ruff moved, winced, and grabbed his ribs. His hand came away wet with blood. He knelt down beside his father. Justin stared up at them, his face as bluish-gray as Georgia slate. His eyelids fluttered and he tried to speak. A froth of blood bubbled from his mouth and Ruff knew that his father was dying.

"Go away!" Justin moaned. "Go to Aunt Maybelle. Go . . . to . . . the Indian Territory!"

Dixie laid her face on her father's torn chest and wept uncontrollably as Justin expelled his last breath.

Houston emptied his gun uselessly at the retreating Confederates. Then he stared out into the yard at the two dead cavalrymen and, farther out, Captain Denton. The mare that Denton had been riding was trotting toward their barn, whinnying pitiously as it headed for its own stall.

Ruff tore his eyes from Justin's still face. When he tried to stand, a sharp pain made him groan.

"Ruff, you've been hit!" Dixie exclaimed as she looked up, her face streaked with tears and her father's blood.

"It's nothing to worry about."

Houston grabbed Ruff's shirt and ripped it open to study the wound. "You'll live, but I think a rib or two might be broken."

"They wouldn't be the first," Ruff said. He swallowed hard. "What are we going to do about Pa?"

"Bury him beside our mother and brother," Houston said, his voice tighter than piano wire. "We'll bury him and the other dead so that no one will ever know what happened today."

"But the ones who escaped . . . they'll know!"

Houston gazed up the empty road. "Lieutenant Pike—if he even was a lieutenant—has probably bled to death by now. The other two . . . well, I suppose I could go after them and make sure they never talked. . . ."

"No!" Dixie cried. "There has been enough killing!"

"She's right," Ruff said. "You're not going to hunt our own boys down and kill them in order to keep this a secret."

Houston started to argue but when he looked into their faces, he changed his mind. "All right," he sighed, "we let them go and hope they never say a word or that they're killed by the Union army before they can tell folks about this fight."

"But it was a *fair* fight!" Ruff protested. "Lieutenant Pike was the first one to open fire. We either killed them or they killed us."

"That's right," Houston said, "but we both know that isn't how the story will be told. Those cavalrymen will say that *we* started the fight and shot those two officers in cold blood. What else *could* they say?"

Ruff understood. "You're right," he conceded, "they couldn't tell the truth."

"Of course they couldn't! And if they talk, we can forget about ever coming home." Houston placed his hand on Ruff's shoulder and that of his sister. "If word of this gets out," he said, "it'll be just like Lieutenant Pike said: we'll be hunted down like rabid dogs."

Dixie and Ruff both nodded their heads as the terrible truth sank in. They were alive, but according to a strictly held Southern code of honor and the fanatic patriotism of their Tennessee neighbors, if news of this fight was ever told, they might as well be dead.

Southerner killing Southerner—in times like this—was an unforgivable sin.

NINE

It was dark before they could finish digging Justin's grave. The Negroes helped and some cried openly when Justin was lowered into the cold Tennessee earth. Ruff stood between his brother and his sister while Marilee and her people sang gospel songs. Songs so sweet and sad they sent shivers rifling up and down Ruff's back. Songs so beautiful and melodic, they brought tears to his eyes.

When the singing was done, Marilee handed Houston a worn Bible. "I suspect your father would like you to read a few words over his grave."

Houston was not an especially religous man, but he knew that Marilee was right. Justin himself had read from the Good Book when they'd buried their mother, and most recently again when they'd buried Mason. Too embarrassed to ask what might be appropriate, Houston simply selected a passage at random. He began to read, his words halting, his voice troubled and sad.

"Psalm Sixty-seven. 'God be merciful unto us, and bless us; and cause his face to shine upon us. That Thy way may be known upon earth, Thy saving health among all nations.' "

Houston's hands began to shake and he tried to go on but failed, eyes dropping a few lines and lips whispering, " 'God shall bless us; and all the ends of the earth shall fear Him.' "

He shuddered and Marilee took the Bible. "I know he could hear you, Houston. I know you made your father proud."

"My father was a good man and he loved us as much as he loved his horses." Houston looked to Ruff, then to Dixie and finally to the newly freed slaves. When he spoke, his voice was loud enough for everyone to hear.

"He loved all of us. We were family. These are hard and dangerous times. But with God's help and protection, we will prevail."

Houston's voice hardened. "It says in the Bible that we should fear God, and I guess that we should. But Heaven help the Yankee that tries to keep what is left of the Ballous from making a fresh start after this war! Or of continuing to breed and improve the finest line of Thoroughbred horses on earth!"

Dixie took her brother's arm. She had never seen him so upset. Of all her brothers, Houston was the least likely to reveal his pain or disappointment. He hadn't shed a tear even when they'd buried Mason.

Houston allowed himself to be led back to the house, leaving Ruff to fill in the grave. Without a word or gesture, the ex-bondsmen took up the shovels and slowly, reverently, filled the grave.

"We'll be leavin' come mo'nin'," Marilee said. "Probably never see you again, Massa Rufus."

Ruff tried to dredge up a smile. "Marilee, you don't have to call me or anyone else 'massa' again. We're all the same now."

"I suspect that's so, but it don't *feel* right yet."

"Someday, I think it will," Ruff said. "Good-bye."

In the early morning, when Ruff and Dixie hitched the mules to their wagon, Marilee and the rest of the Ballous' former slaves came by and waited until they were gone. Most had never been in the house and it had been decided that Marilee would parcel out the furniture. After that, Ruff hoped that they would be able to cart it away before the Union army arrived.

By ten o'clock, the wagon was loaded and they were ready to depart. They spent a few quiet minutes beside the graves and then, remembering how Justin had intended to leave no sign of burial, leveled the mounds and scattered leaves across the cemetery.

"When we come back," Ruff said, mounting High Man, "we'll have new headstones engraved for all three. And we'll build a pretty picket fence around the graves, too."

"We'll make some changes," Houston agreed. "Do some of the things that Pa had been planning on doing for years but never quite got around to for one reason or another."

Dixie looked back at the Ballou mansion. There were other homes in Tennessee more stately and impressive, but this one, with its wide veranda, its gables and pillars, would always be, for her, the most beautiful.

"I pray the Yankees don't put the torch to it," she whispered.

Ruff started to say something, then changed his mind and rode away in silence without looking back. He could feel the pull of the mansion; it almost seemed to beg him and the last of the Ballous to stay, to fight and even to die if necessary.

It is just a house, he thought, just mortar and wood and stone. What must be saved is my father's dream and vision—his life's work. So ride on! Save what can be saved and put behind you what cannot.

The two young stallions tied to the back of the wagon twisted their necks and bugled a farewell to Wildwood Farm. The mares tied to the sides of the wagon nickered anxiously and rolled their eyes as Houston took the lines.

"He-yah, mules!"

Art and Jenny, the mules, leaned into the harness and the wagon jolted forward. Dixie rode the strongest mare and when Ruff glanced sideways at her, he saw that her eyes were leaking silent tears of farewell. At the bend of the road just south of their property line, Dixie twisted around in her saddle and Ruff heard an involuntary sob escape her lips.

"Don't look back, Dixie," he said. "It just makes leaving harder."

"Do you think we will ever return?"

"I don't know. Maybe. But maybe we'll find better land in the West."

"I can't imagine that we will ever find any place to live so beautiful as Tennessee."

Houston overheard the conversation and said, "Could be you're right, Dixie. The thing of it is, change is never easy. If this war hadn't come about, we might have all lived our lives just a few miles from home, raising Thoroughbreds and maybe even children. Now we're going to be tested like our horses were always tested on the racetracks."

"And what if we're not winners?" Dixie asked.

"Well," Houston said after a long consideration, "then we need to know that, too. Not every horse can streak across the finish line first. But those that try and finish the race as best they can still deserve credit."

"Credit?" Dixie shook her head. "Second place is nothing. Do you think that Jefferson Davis or the Confederacy will get 'credit' when our side finally lays down its arms? Will all the dear, dead Johnny Rebs get 'credit'?"

Dixie's voice shook with bitterness. "Of course not! All the spoils go to the winners—on the racetrack, on the battlefield . . . or in life."

Ruff didn't know how completely he could agree with his sister's harsh opinion. "Seems to me that some folks that haven't much in the way of goods or money are happier than those that are rich. Take Pa for example: he wasn't near as rich as them cotton farmers down south in Alabama. Or even some of his friends in Chattanooga. But he was a whole lot happier. That's because he was doing what he wanted to do."

"And so will we," Houston said in a gruff voice. "Ain't a damn thing to stop us."

Dixie looked at her two big brothers as if they were prattling schoolboys and she was their teacher. "Are you both forgetting about the war?"

"No," Ruff said, "but it can't last much longer. And I think we ought to be damn grateful just to be alive and have the foundation stock to rebuild our Thoroughbreds' bloodlines."

"You always were easy to please," Dixie said.

Ruff gave up on his kid sister. Dixie could be awfully contrary when she got into a certain mood like the one she was in right now. When that happened, you could talk sense to her all day and night and she'd stay mulish. It was a waste of breath to try to turn her head around so Ruff concentrated on keeping a sharp eye out for any Yankees that might be running loose. If they accidentally crossed the path of a couple of Yank snipers, then this whole stupid conversation about winners and losers would be irrelevant.

"Ruff?" Dixie asked about an hour later while they were riding together out in front of the wagon.

"What?"

"Do you think he lived?"

"Who?"

"Lieutenant Pike."

"I don't know. Probably not. He was losing a lot of blood from his neck when he disappeared up the road."

"I hope he's roasting in hell!"

Ruff glanced sideways at his sister. "That's no way for a lady to talk."

"I'm not a lady and I never will be," Dixie said. "And if Lieutenant Pike didn't bleed to death, I want to shoot the murderin' son of a bitch myself for killing Pa."

Her language was shocking. Ruff wondered if he knew his sister at all anymore. He had before the war. They'd always been close confidants and friends. But the deaths of John, Micha, Mason, and now their father had changed everything. Dixie was no longer just a headstrong girl talented with horses. Ruff worried that his kid sister was on the verge of becoming a hard, bitter young woman.

That deeply saddened Ruff. He had danced and laughed with plenty of Southern belles and even kissed his share. Not one of them talked or viewed life like Dixie.

"Don't you remember what our mother said about hate?"

"You mean how it is really love turned around?"

"Yes."

Dixie scoffed. "Mother might have been a saint, but she wasn't always right. I didn't buy a word of that love-hate business the first time I heard it and I don't think I ever will."

Ruff said nothing.

"Well," Dixie demanded, "do you?"

"I don't know," Ruff admitted, "but if our mother said it, I guess it bears some consideration."

Dixie stared at him. "You're too naive," she said. "You're brave but you're too naive. If Houston and I don't keep a sharp eye out, some Yankee is going to shoot you dead."

Ruff was offended. "I'd be a job for 'em, Dixie."

"Oh yeah, well what about those bullet-cracked ribs? And that missing earlobe?"

"They'll all mend," Ruff said, "and just remember that, thanks to me, Lieutenant Pike is probably dancing in the fires of hell."

"Horses coming up from behind!" Houston shouted up to them.

Ruff reined his stallion around, dragging out his Colt and charging back to the wagon with Dixie. The stallion was dancing with excitement and Ruff's heart had already begun to hammer. Houston had pulled the wagon off to the side of the road, set the brake, and ducked down behind the piano.

"Hold your fire!" Dixie shouted.

A carriage was racing at them like a runaway train. Ruff could see that the four-horse team was coated with lather and he heard the crack of the buggy whip that was being used on their sweaty backs. The driver was a big, florid-faced man and beside him was a woman of about twenty, beautiful but obviously terrified.

"What the hell is the matter with him?" Ruff shouted. "Is he crazy?"

"Hey!" Houston shouted as the heavy carriage thundered past. "Hold up there!"

But the man just kept whipping the team. Ruff and Dixie exchanged glances and then raced after them. It took Ruff and Dixie a half mile to overtake the carriage and another half mile to finally pull the lead horses to a standstill.

"Damn you, let go of those horses!" the driver shouted.

Ruff released the bridle and rode back to the carriage. He had never seen this couple before, but it was obvious that he was dealing with a man who was accustomed to giving orders.

"Get out of our way!" the driver yelled at Dixie, who had ridden up to block the carriage's progress.

Ruff took the lines in his fist. His father had taught them never to allow men to mistreat animals, even if it meant a fight. Well, this team was ready to collapse and Ruff was ready to fight.

"Mister, you're going to kill this team if you don't stop running them."

"If I do, that's my damned business, not yours! Now, tell that girl to get out of our way!"

The man waved his buggy whip and his horses bolted forward in fear. Ruff was almost pulled from his saddle trying to hold the lines.

"Let go, damn you!"

The driver lashed out with the whip and it struck Ruff on the cheek, stinging like crazy. Without any thought, he threw himself into the carriage. The man swore and tried to drive the butt of his whip into Ruff's eyes. That made Ruff all the angrier and he slammed his head into the man's face, hearing the driver's nose pop.

"Ahhh!" the man shouted as they both toppled out of the carriage. Unfortunately, the big man landed on top. Ruff took two sledgehammering blows to the face.

"Hook him!" Dixie shouted. "Hook him!"

Ruff's mind was just clear enough to know what Dixie meant. He whipped his legs up and hooked his heels into the fellow's neck, then dragged him over backward.

"Thataway, now hit him! Kick him! Punch him!"

They both struggled to their feet. Ruff ducked a round-house punch and drove his fist into the man's gut. To his surprise and disappointment, the man did not crumple. Instead, he punched so hard Ruff went down to one knee.

Dixie jumped off her horse but before she could compli-cate things, the man kicked at Ruff, who managed to duck and grab his boot. He surged to his feet, throwing the leg overhead, and the big man crashed to earth. Ruff landed on his chest with doubled knees and the man's cheeks bellowed out. Ruff punched him him three times and went limp.

"Thataway!" Dixie cried, grabbing Ruff and supporting him. "For a minute, I thought you were going to let him whip you."

"For a minute, I thought he *was* going to whip me," Ruff gasped, dragging in deep lungfuls of breath. "And . . ."

Whatever Ruff was going to say was instantly forgotten when the beautiful woman in the carriage cocked the ham-mer of a derringer and said, "Get away from him or I'll shoot you both!"

Ruff blinked and Dixie's face flamed. "Why . . ."

"I mean it!" she ordered. "Help him back into this car-riage and get out of our way!"

Ruff stared down at the man lying at his feet. "He was bound to kill these horses, ma'am. I can't allow that, so if you're of a mind to shoot, shoot me, not my sister."

Dixie put her hand on the holstered Colt resting on her hip. "I'll tell you this, lady, if you shoot my brother, I'll drill you square."

The woman swallowed. She could hear Houston yelling at the mules as he hurried to catch up. Seeming to make a decision, she said, "You're Southerners, aren't you?"

"Yes," Ruff said, "but . . ."

"I've *got* to reach Ashley, Alabama! It's a matter of vital importance to the South."

"What the hell is going on!" Houston shouted, jumping off their wagon and charging up to the carriage with his gun in his fist. "Who"—Houston lowered his gun and his voice when he saw the beautiful woman—"are you?"

She looked at the three of them and then down at the driver of her carriage. Turning back to Houston, she lowered her derringer and smiled. "My name is Candice."

Houston removed his hat with a flourish. He holstered his gun and introduced himself, then, as an afterthought, Ruff and Dixie.

"Candice what?" Dixie demanded.

The woman turned her gaze on Dixie and studied her like an insect before explaining to Houston, "Sir, my last name is not important."

"Probably doesn't have one," Dixie muttered.

Ruff himself was a little dazzled by the woman. She had strawberry blond hair, peaches-and-cream skin, and beautiful green eyes. Her figure was . . . well, voluptuous to put it modestly.

"I think," Houston said, taking in the scene at a glance and extending his hand up to the young woman, "that we seem to have had a very unfortunate misunderstanding."

"Exactly so," Candice said. She took Houston's hand and allowed herself to be helped down from the carriage. "But poor Mr. Farnum! Did you really need to hurt him so badly?"

Ruff pressed his hand hard against his ribs, which were beginning to ache fiercely. His face was numb and he knew that it would be swollen and misshapen by the blows he'd taken from the big driver.

"Miss, exactly who is Mr. Farnum?" he demanded.

"My friend and protector, of course," Candice said, "and we are on our way to Ashley to deliver a message of the most vital military importance. Can you please help? "

She turned her green eyes to Houston, and Ruff saw his brother nod his head, then heard him say, "We'll do everything possible to assist you. But we can't allow those horses to be run to death."

"Exactly what is this 'vital' message that you have to deliver?" Dixie asked.

Candice raised her eyebrows. "My dear . . . girl, we are talking about a very important military secret. I have a message for Major Pritchard himself!"

"I never even heard of the man." Clearly, Dixie was not impressed.

Candice reflected astonishment. "Dear girl! Major Pritchard may not yet be famous, but I assure you that he will be *if* I am allowed to deliver this most important message without further delay."

Dixie snorted with disgust. "Houston, would you stuff your eyeballs back into your head and use it for something beside a hat rack! This woman is a fraud!"

"What!"

Dixie took a threatening step toward the woman. "You heard me!"

Houston had to jump in between the pair. "Now stop it! Both of you!"

"Ask her to show you the message!" Dixie demanded. "Or something to prove what she says."

"I'm sure Miss Candice is . . ."

"Ask her," Ruff said, kneeling to riffle through the coat pockets of the man he'd just knocked out cold.

"You won't find any identification on either of us," Candice said coolly, "assuming that you are not looking for money."

"Of course not." Houston looked apologetic. "But in times like this, we can't afford to trust anyone. So, if you would please be a little more specific, it would be appreciated."

"Aw, for cripes—"

"Hush, Dixie!"

The woman drew a deep breath. "All right," she began, "we are Southern spies fleeing Chattanooga with information that is of vital importance to the Confederacy. And unless you release me and help me put dear Mr. Farnum into the carriage so that we can reach Major Pritchard, you may well become responsible for the slaughter of thousands of our troops."

"Ask her why she is killing those horses!" Dixie demanded.

Candice didn't have to be asked. "Why? Because we are being pursued by a Yankee patrol."

Ruff and Houston both whirled to look back up the road, and Houston said, "How far?"

"Not far at all," Candice replied, her eyes daring them to challenge her assertion. "And if you don't believe me, just detain Mr. Farnum and myself another quarter hour and I'll guarantee that we will all be shot."

Ruff looked to Dixie and saw that fight had been replaced by doubt. Ruff said, "Perhaps we ought to do as the lady suggests and buy ourselves a little time?"

"Good idea," Houston said hastily. "There's a stream just up ahead. I think we had better drive our wagon on up it and hide."

"But what of this carriage?"

"The Yankees will be following its tracks," Ruff explained. "If those tracks didn't come through the stream, they'd soon find us."

"So what can we do?" Candice demanded.

"I'll drive it on," Ruff said. "There's no other choice but to hope I come upon a town where there are many fresh wheel tracks. Maybe I can hide it until the patrol gives up the chase."

"But her team of horses is played out," Dixie argued.

Ruff went to examine the team more closely. The four horses were badly winded but they would soon recover.

"They'll be all right. I'll start off slow, then pick up the pace when they've recovered their wind." Ruff turned to his brother. "Help me get Farnum into the carriage. We'll all meet here later tonight."

"I don't like this," Houston said as they tossed Farnum into the carriage and Ruff climbed on board.

"Until we sort things out, there are no other choices," Ruff said, picking up the lines and forcing the winded team on down the road.

He glanced back over his shoulder to see that Houston was already helping Candice into their wagon.

"I still don't believe her!" Dixie shouted up to him.

Ruff expelled a deep breath. He didn't know what to believe. It seemed impossible that such a stunning young woman as Candice could really be a Southern spy on the run. Maybe she was lying. But why? Ruff had no idea, but since Houston was far more experienced with beautiful women, he would let his older brother sort that one out.

TEN

"*Pssst! Psssst,* Houston!"

"What, dammit!"

Dixie motioned her brother over behind their wagon, where they could talk without being overheard. "I still don't believe a word that woman has said! Do you?"

"Why should she lie?"

"How should I know! But if you're fool enough to trust Candice, we'll lose everything."

Houston glanced back over his shoulder. "Listen," he said in a low voice, "we've got to get our wagon up that stream right now! If she's lying, it'll be easy enough to tell because there won't be a Yankee patrol flying down this road in the next few minutes. Now, stop being so damned suspicious and let's get out of here."

"I don't like it," Dixie said before she mounted her horse.

Houston grumbled something and then hauled himself up to the wagon seat beside the young woman.

"Hang on, Miss Candice," he said, releasing the brake and slapping the lines smartly against the rumps of Art and Jenny. The mules, unaccustomed to being stung into action, brayed their displeasure, but when Houston slapped them again, they laid back their ears and did their particular imitation of running.

Dixie rode along behind the wagon, every few minutes twisting around to see if there really had been a Yankee patrol charging after that carriage. As far as she was concerned, this whole business smacked of deception and she wouldn't have trusted Miss Candice any farther than she could have thrown Mr. Farnum. Furthermore, Dixie wasn't a bit pleased about how Houston was laying the leather to poor old Art and Jenny. Her father had set quite a store by that pair, and if he'd have been alive to see the way that Houston was making them run . . . well, he'd have been the one who would be laying on the leather.

When they finally reached the stream, Houston swung the mules off the road and went splashing up the shallow water. It was good thing that the streambed was gravelly rather than sandy or they'd have sunk to the hubs and been in a bad fix.

"Hi-yahhh!" Houston bellowed over and over as the two powerful mules bucked and lunged up the stream until the wagon was just out of sight of the road, beyond a bend.

"All right!" Dixie shouted. "That's far enough."

But Houston drove them up and out of the stream to dry ground. Art and Jenny were blowing like a blacksmith's bellows, heads down, eyeballs distended, and coats glistening with sweat and water.

"Dammit, Houston," Dixie cried, jumping down, tying her horse and then running over to comfort the mules, "you didn't need to be so awful with them! Why, if—"

"Hush!" he hissed. "Listen."

Dixie froze. Her eyes widened and then she spun around. Through the trees, she saw a Union patrol gallop into sight, and when it crossed the stream, sheets of water exploded into the air. The riders passed so quickly they were a blur, but they were a very *long* blur.

Dixie squeezed her eyes shut and opened them to stare into Candice's defiant green eyes.

"Satisfied now, Miss Ballou?"

Dixie managed to dip her chin to indicate that she was, indeed, quite satisfied.

Houston removed his hat and grinned at the young woman. "Miss, they'd have caught us flat-footed if you and Farnum hadn't overtaken us first. I don't know what would have happened to us if you had not come along."

"You'd have tried to fight and you'd have been shot down," Candice said. "Now, will you please help me get a message to Major Pritchard?"

"I will," Houston said, looking sternly at Dixie. "Well?"

"All right, I will, too," she heard herself say, "but not until Ruff is back safely with us."

"He'll probably be overtaken before he can reach the next town," Candice said without a trace of regret.

"Then we need to help him!"

"*You* may need to help him," Candice said to them both. "I won't. My responsibility is to reach Major Pritchard."

"Well what about Mr. Farnum?"

"I can't help him, either," Candice said. "They are entirely on their own and they'll need luck if they have any chance of surviving this day."

Dixie was outraged. "I'll be damned if I'm going to just allow them to be overtaken and killed!"

She whirled and ran over to untie High Man, who would be a lot faster reaching Ashley than the mare she had been riding.

"Dixie!" Houston shouted. "Dixie, don't you dare go after them!"

But Dixie wasn't listening. She sent High Man charging up the stream and when she hit the road, she turned the tall horse loose and let the old Thoroughbred run like the wind. She had never raced High Man and she was astonished at how fast the horse could still move. With any luck at all, she might even overtake the Yankee patrol and . . . that would be a disaster!

Dixie pulled the Thoroughbred up but High Man fought for its head, wanting to take the bit in its teeth and run.

And as she galloped along, trying to hold the stallion down so that she could conserve its strength for whatever might happen in the hours to come, Dixie fretted about Ruff. Had he been able to reach the next town before being overtaken by the Yankees? And even if he had, what had become of the carriage? Ruff couldn't hide its tracks. The patrol would find him and . . .

"Stop it!" Dixie cried out to herself. "Or you'll go crazy!"

At the sound of her voice, High Man's ears twitched back and forth as he devoured the forest road that carried them deeper into the northwest corner of Georgia.

Ruff recalled that the next town he'd see was called Pineville but it was nothing more than a tavern, a combination livery-blacksmith shop, general mercantile, and a few stores surrounded by half a dozen or so cabins and farms. He'd once taken a fancy to a Pineville girl named Esther Drury, whose father was the town blacksmith and liveryman. Mr. Drury had tried hard to promote the romance, obviously hoping that his daughter would marry upward into the prominent Ballou family and that he would get all the horseshoeing business at Wildwood Farm.

Esther had disappointed everyone when she ran off to Atlanta with a traveling drummer and where, last Ruff had heard, she had jilted the drummer and married a baker. Esther's younger sister, Flora, had written Ruff several not-so-subtle letters indicating that she was more than willing to replace her sister in Ruff's affections.

Maybe Flora would help, Ruff thought as he drove into Pineville, looking for someone who might be able to explain to him how he was going to hide a carriage and what he could do with the still-unconscious Mr. Farnum.

But this day, Pineville seemed almost deserted except for a few old men sitting under the porch of Anson's Mercantile. Ruff wheeled the carriage around behind the blacksmith's livery barn and shop. He could hear Mr. Drury working on his forge. Ruff jumped down from the carriage and raced inside. Mr. Drury looked up, his square face bathed in sweat, hammer raised over his anvil.

"Mr. Ballou?"

Ruff nodded. It had been at least a year since he'd visited Esther and he was glad to see that the blacksmith still remembered him.

"Mr. Drury, there may be a Yankee patrol on its way down from Chattanooga. And they may be after the carriage I just parked behind your shop."

The hammer fell from the blacksmith's hand. "What?"

"You heard me. I've got a Southern spy in the carriage named Farnum and he's knocked out cold. You got to help us before we are found!"

"Get out of here!" Drury yelled, fists balling up. He glanced sideways and saw the carriage and the badly lathered team of horses. "Go!"

"But . . ."

Drury grabbed up his hammer, and Ruff's hand dropped to his gun butt, which caused the blacksmith to freeze in his tracks.

"Just go," Drury implored. "This won't be the first Union patrol that's come through Pineville but so far they've left us alone. I won't have you changing that."

"But I can't just let them have Farnum!"

"Then hide the carriage in the forest somewheres!"

"Will you take care of the man if I leave him here? I'll be back for him in a few minutes."

Drury hesitated and Ruff's anger flared. "He's a Southern spy! We can't just let the Yanks capture the man!"

"All right. Let's get him out of the carriage. Quickly now!"

Drury wasn't tall but he was ox strong and in such a panic that Ruff just stood to one side and let the blacksmith haul Farnum out of the carriage and take him inside, where he threw the unconscious man onto a pile of bedding straw.

"What happened to his nose? Did they already try and beat information out of him?" Drury asked as he ran to grab a pitchfork.

Ruff didn't want to explain. "I'll drive the carriage on

through town. If they come, fire a shot of warning so I don't get overtaken."

Drury nodded grimly and began to pitch straw over Farnum. "Get out of here!"

Ruff sprinted to the carriage. He snatched up the lines and sent the team lunging into their traces. The carriage slewed around in the livery yard and almost overturned before Ruff could get it lined out down the road. He had not traveled more than two hundred yards, however, when he heard a lone gunshot.

Ruff leaned out from the seat of the carriage to see a pack of bluecoats charging into the opposite end of town.

"Holy hog fat!" he shouted, lashing the poor team.

At the first bend in the road, Ruff took a final backward glance and, sure enough, the Union patrol was pouring through Pineville, hot on his trail. Ruff figured he had about three minutes' lead time before he'd be in the Yankees' pistol range.

There was no choice but to pick a spot and jump while he was still shielded from view by the bend in the road. Ruff dropped the lines and picked a landing covered by soft, marshy ground and tall tules. He jumped.

Ruff struck the marshy ground, plowing up a good twenty feet of tules. Spitting and choking, clawing and slipping, he came to his feet and began to push his way deeper into the marsh. His breath was coming so fast he could not hear the sound of the Union horses but he knew they would be flying past him in a moment or two—if he was lucky.

Ruff scrambled onward, breath coming in fiery gasps, legs cramping and ribs protesting fiercely. At last, when he could run no more, he collapsed in the marsh and struggled to catch his breath and gather his scattered senses.

He listened intently for the sounds of pursuit but all he heard was a farmer's dog barking just a little bit off to the east. Ruff came to his feet. He was covered from head to toe with mud and torn tules and thistles. He could only imagine what kind of impression he would make if he were discovered.

His Army Colt was hopelessly fouled with mud and completely useless. Ruff decided that his only chance was to circle around behind Pineville and sneak back to Drury's blacksmith shop. Maybe by now Farnum had regained his senses and, together, they could come up with a plan on how to salvage things.

Ruff wiped the mud from his hands as best he could and waded on through the marsh. Back on solid ground it took him twenty minutes to return to the blacksmith shop without being seen.

"Mr. Drury?" he whispered. "Mr. Drury?"

There was no answer. Ruff sneaked into the livery. He hurried over to the pile of bedding straw and reached inside to grab Mr. Farnum. Only it wasn't Mr. Farnum—it was Mr. Drury! And he had a knife buried in his chest.

"Freeze!" ordered a voice from behind.

Ruff's hand instinctively clawed for the gun on his hip, but before he could tear it free from his holster, Ruff felt a terrible pain that originated just behind his right ear.

He pitched over unconscious to cover poor, dead Mr. Drury.

ELEVEN

Dixie finally managed to get High Man settled into a nice easy canter by the time she entered Pineville. She arrived to find everyone milling about in the street.

"What's wrong?" she asked an apple-cheeked woman holding an infant to her breast.

"I don't know! Someone said that a Union cavalry patrol just galloped through our town. I was feeding my baby and didn't see anything. And then there was this shot! I came outside and so did all my neighbors."

Dixie guided High Man through the street, looking for someone who might be able to tell her if they saw the carriage race through Pineville just ahead of the Yankees.

Suddenly, she heard a scream and saw a girl only a few years older than herself stagger out of a livery. "It's my father!" the girl wailed. "He's been murdered by Rufus Ballou!"

Dixie's heart stopped. She whirled High Man around and drove him right through the livery barn doors. Diving off the stallion, she saw Ruff collapsed unconscious across a man with a knife protruding from his broad chest. Ruff was covered from head to toe with black mud and, had it not been for his height, she'd never have even recognized him.

"Oh lordy," she whispered, "we're in for it now!"

There were two or three gawking men inside the barn. When Dixie forced her way between them to drop beside her brother, they tried to grab her arm and pull her aside.

109

Dixie whirled on them, drawing her Colt.

"Git!"

The men recoiled and backpedaled to the door, where one managed to bluster, "My name is Mr. Ott, I'm on Pineville's town council and I *demand* to know the meaning of this, young lady!"

"This is my brother and I'm getting him out of here before that damned Yankee cavalry patrol returns."

"Not until we've gotten some answers!" Ott swore, almost jumping up and down in his extreme agitation. "Did your brother kill Mr. Drury?"

Dixie shoved her Navy Colt out to full arm's length and, using both hands, managed to cock the hammer. Ott and his companions threw their hands overhead and the councilman pleaded, "Don't shoot! We're all family men!"

"I won't kill any of you, but I'm not going to give my brother up to the Yankees or you and your damned town council. So stay back."

"Young lady," Ott warned, "if you use that gun you'll be very sorry indeed! I demand that you hand over that man."

"Use your head, Mr. Ott! How could my brother have stabbed a man to death when an ordinary idiot can see he's been knocked unconscious? Find the man that did this to my brother and you'll have your killer."

"You've no proof of that!"

Dixie reached down and touched the bloody goose egg on the back of Ruff's head. She held her hand up so they could see that Ruff was badly injured. "Look! Someone tried to split Ruff's skull open! *That's* our proof."

Mr. Ott and the other townspeople stared at her bloodied fingers, then turned and began to argue among themselves. Dixie twisted around to slap her brother's face. "Ruff, wake up! We've got to get out of here!"

Ruff groaned. Dixie kept slapping his face until his eyes finally popped open. "Leave me alone."

"I can't. Wake up and let's go before it's too late."

Ruff didn't want to wake up but Dixie wouldn't stop slapping his face until he was forced to his feet. It was right about then that his eyes focused on Mr. Drury with the knife sticking in his chest and everything came flooding back to nearly overpower him.

"Ruff, let's go," Dixie whispered urgently, reading the shock and confusion in her brother's dazed expression.

Ruff nodded dumbly, and with her gun still clenched in her fist, Dixie led her wobbly brother over to High Man. The Thoroughbred stallion nuzzled Ruff affectionately.

"Put your foot in the stirrup," Dixie ordered. "I'll help you into the saddle."

"We demand some explanation!" Ott cried. "As Pineville's—"

Dixie spun and drew a bead on the man's bowler. One shot and the bowler disappeared through the door. The crowd outside scattered, followed by Mr. Ott and his three companions.

"Here," Dixie said, placing Ruff's hand on the saddle horn, "you can do it. Easy, High Man. This is no time for you to start dancin' or prancin'."

The stallion seemed to understand and despite the tension and gun smoke, the Thoroughbred was steady. Ruff hauled himself into the saddle and then dropped his arm and Dixie clasped it. It was a trick they had practiced as children, and the stallion whirled as if on cue, catapulting Dixie into the air to land behind her brother.

"Let's ride!"

"Rufus!" a pretty young woman cried, heartbroken, as Ruff and Dixie blasted out through the barn door, scattering the citizens of Pineville like a covey of quail. "Why did you kill my father?"

Ruff tried to shout back to Flora that he hadn't killed anyone. But his head was spinning and his tongue seemed to plug his mouth. It was all that he could do to hang onto the reins and High Man's mane.

"Wrong direction!" Dixie cried, reaching around from

behind and wrestling for control of the reins. "This way we run head on into that Yankee patrol!"

Together, they got High Man turned back to the north and, this time, the old Thoroughbred took the bit in his long yellow teeth and ran for all he was worth.

Dixie clung to her brother, afraid that he might pitch off sideways in a faint. Or that High Man might lose his footing and hurl them to their destruction against the road's hard surface.

They galloped for nearly three miles, the old racehorse gradually slowing until he was winded and willing to walk.

"Ruff?"

"Yeah?" he asked, tenderly probing the goose egg on the back of his head.

"Are you still of a right mind?"

"I . . . I think so."

"Who killed Mr. Drury?"

"I don't know."

Dixie laid her head against her brother's muddy shoulder. "I knew it wasn't you. Was it a Yankee soldier?"

"Maybe. Maybe not."

"Who else could have done such a terrible thing?"

"Mr. Farnum," Ruff heard himself say. "I think Mr. Farnum stabbed Mr. Drury to death."

"But why?"

"I haven't a clue," Ruff said, shaking the cobwebs out of his aching head, "but if I ever come across the man, you can be sure I'll find out."

They rode High Man back to the stream and then through the water to their wagon. Everything was just as Dixie had left it except for one thing.

"They're gone," she whispered, after a frantic search. "Houston and that . . . that woman are gone!"

Ruff was on his knees in the stream trying to wash marsh mud out of his ears, eyes, and even his mouth. He looked up. "Gone?"

"Yes!"

"On foot?"

"Of course not!" Dixie cried. "They took one of the young stallions and our best mare!"

Ruff dunked his head back in the cold stream and worked a mouthful of water around and around before he spat it out. Dixie looked ready to explode.

"Don't worry," he managed to say. "As soon as I can get my brain pieced back together, we'll come up with a plan to find them. Houston knows what he is doing. He'll probably return soon."

Dixie sat down in the stream and began to cry.

"Aw, stop it!" Ruff pleaded. "He's going to be all right! I swear he will."

"It's not him that I'm worried about."

"Oh. Well, then our horses will be fine, too. Nobody in their right mind is going to hurt them."

Dixie scrubbed the tears from her eyes. "We're making an awful mess of things. If Pa were still alive to see the miserable fix we're in right now, he'd be damned disgusted with us."

Ruff started to argue but he just couldn't because he guessed that Dixie was right. Old Justin might not have been disgusted, exactly, but he'd have at least been highly exasperated.

"Houston will be fine, Dixie. Any minute now he'll come riding back on the stallion leading the mare. He probably just took Miss Candice to Ashley in order to find that Major Pritchard. Once he's delivered her safe and sound, he'll hurry back."

"Do you really think so?" she asked hopefully.

"Sure! Why else would he leave?"

"I don't know but I can't imagine Houston leaving our mares untended. And if Mr. Farnum really was a Southern spy, then why would he stab that man from Pineville to death?"

Ruff looked away because he really didn't have a good answer.

• • •

They waited the rest of that day and night and the better part of another day before Ruff and Dixie agreed they could not afford to wait for Houston any longer.

"Do you know how far we have to go to reach Ashley?" Dixie asked her brother as they fed the mules and Thoroughbreds in preparation for leaving their hiding place beside the stream.

"No," Ruff admitted. "I haven't the slightest idea. I guess we'll just keep moving southwest. I'm sure that we'll come across plenty of folks who can tell us where to go."

"In these parts, they'll tell us to go to hell," Dixie said. "I remember Pa saying that he never much cared for Alabama folks."

"We're all Southerners," Ruff said wearily. "That means we're all in this war together. Alabamans understand that, too. They'll help us, Dixie."

Ruff gently pulled his hat on over his goose egg and climbed up onto the seat of the wagon. High Man would have to suffer the indignity of being led at the end of a rope tied to the back of their wagon. Dixie was going to ride the remaining young stallion.

"You ready?" he asked, taking up the lines.

"I'm ready," Dixie said, her expression worried. "But isn't there *some* way we can skirt Pineville? Why, if they recognize us, we could be shot."

"I doubt that," Ruff said, "and the only road into Alabama is this one. That's why we've waited until late this afternoon. So that we can pass through after dark, remember?"

Dixie dipped her chin. "All right, let's go. Ashley might be clear down to the Gulf of Mexico for all we know. Pa always said that distances seem twice as far in Alabama."

Ruff gently slapped the mules with the lines, sending Art and Jenny forward to pick their own best way through the trees and back to the road.

By the time they reached Pineville, darkness had fallen. Ruff could not help but stare at the barred doors on the blacksmith and the livery shops. He passed the Drury house and saw silhouettes behind the shuttered curtains. He felt terrible for poor Flora. Mr. Drury had been a widower and now his remaining daughter would live alone until marriage. Ruff took small comfort in the fact that Flora would be well provided for if the Yankees did not burn the town to the earth after taking everything of value.

They traveled without incident all night, and the next morning, Ruff pulled into a small but well-tended tobacco farm.

"What can we do for you today?" a pleasant-looking man in his late forties asked as he came out on the porch and studied Ruff, Dixie, and their outfit.

"We're traveling to a town called Ashley," Ruff explained. "How far is it?"

"About fifty miles west along the Tennessee River. Little town, but friendly people. Least they were until the Yankees took it last fall."

Ruff's jaw sagged. "It's in Yankee hands?"

"I'm afraid so." The tobacco farmer stepped off his porch, leaving his wife and two small children to stare at Dixie on her fine Thoroughbred stallion. "Damn fine stallion, miss."

"Thank you."

The farmer introduced himself as David Preston, and then walked around the wagon. When he halted beside the right front wheel, he said to Ruff, "You own all this?"

"Me, my sister, and a brother. Why do you ask?"

"I just wondered if you'd consider selling everything real cheap."

The bluntness of the question shocked and annoyed Ruff. "Of course not! Why should I do a fool thing like that?"

"Because the Yanks hold most of the towns between here and Ashley. First one you come to, they're going to confiscate this wagon, horses, and mules anyway. Might as well sell to us for a few dollars to put in your pockets. You can keep the two stallions for runnin'. Keep the mares, too.

They're no good for hitchin' to a plow. I can see that they're Thoroughbred racehorses."

"That they are."

"Fine-looking animals," Preston said, "but useless to me. Still, might be I could take them off your hands for a few dollars."

"They're not for sale," Ruff said. "Nothing we have is for sale at any price."

The farmer shrugged. "Sorry to hear that. The Yanks will be real happy, though, if you understand what I mean."

Ruff glanced over at his sister, whose face was a brittle mask. He turned back to the farmer. "I know what you mean, but we'll take our chances with the Yankees."

Preston laughed.

"What's so funny!" Ruff demanded.

"Oh," the farmer said, rolling a cigarette and then lighting it very deliberately. "Just the way you talk."

"What's wrong with my talk?"

"You talk fine. I meant what was funny was you saying that 'you'd take your chances.' "

The farmer expelled twin streams of tobacco smoke through his nostrils. He was an angular sort, with bib overalls and sharp, penetrating eyes. "You see, mister, what you *don't* see is that you have no chances. Anyone on the road is fair game. And if I had a pretty sister and some fine horses, I'd sure go to ground."

Ruff felt an overpowering urge to jump down and jam that cigarette down Preston's throat. He felt his hands tremble and yet he knew that the farmer was just trying to warn him of the grave danger they would face on the way to Ashley.

"Let's go," Ruff said stiffly to his sister as he lifted the lines.

"No, wait." Dixie chewed her lower lip for a minute, then said to the farmer, "Mr. Preston, these mules are only four years old. They're as fine a team as there is anywhere in the South."

"Dixie!"

She ignored her brother. "And the wagon was made in Memphis by J. B. Atherton and Brothers. I'm sure that you've heard of their fine reputation. And inside rests my mother's beautiful piano. My father had it sent all the way down from Boston."

"Dixie, what in the hell has gotten into you!" Ruff stormed.

She finally looked over at him. "Ruff, we haven't got a prayer with that wagon. If we try to hang on to it and all of Mother's furniture, we'll lose it anyway. And we'll lose the Thoroughbreds, too—not to mention our lives."

Ruff's throat worked silently.

"She's right," Preston said cheerfully. "You *will* lose everything to the Yankees. And if you try to hang on to it, the Yankee soldiers will kill you for certain."

Ruff jumped down from the wagon and started walking very rapidly. He heard Dixie gallop up beside him, and when they were out in the fields far enough so they could not be overheard, he stopped and whirled around.

"Mother's furniture was supposed to be yours someday. All of it! You're her only daughter and now . . . now you want to practically give it away. What's gotten into you!"

Dixie dismounted and touched his arm. "I'll tell you what," she said in a quiet voice. "We're riding into deep trouble and all that matters to me is saving you and our Thoroughbreds. That's all. Next to that, the furniture doesn't matter."

"Haven't you forgotten Houston?"

"He'll be fine," Dixie said. "I know it and you know it. He's got nothing to lose and he knows how to talk or fight his way out of trouble. And even if he has to run to save his life, he might not be happy, but run he will."

Dixie met her brother's eyes. "Ruff, that's what we got to do to save our horses—run!"

"But Mother's things. It's all that we have left of her and Pa. Without—"

"If we are caught, we'll lose them anyway," Dixie said, shaking her head. "And we'd lose the horses. Next to our lives, it's Father's horses that are most important."

Ruff jammed his big hands into his pockets. "You know I don't give a damn about the furniture. It was for you, Dixie."

"I want to sell it. It's like a chain we're dragging around. It'll pull us down."

Ruff stared into her black eyes a moment and then he found himself nodding his head.

"All right," he sighed, "let's see what kind of an offer we can get out of this farmer. But I won't *give* it away! We'll go on to another farm and dicker until we get a fair price. You hear me?"

He was angry but that dissipated when Dixie reached up and kissed his cheek. "You let me do the dickering, Ruff. I'm better at it."

He had to grin. "Yeah, I'm no good thataway."

"Maybe not," she said, "but you're the finest horsemen I or anyone else has ever seen."

Ruff swelled up a little to hear his kid sister say that. Dixie was a vixen, but at times like this, he loved her dearly.

TWELVE

Houston rode stirrup to stirrup with the beautiful Candice, and even after almost fifty miles of dodging Union patrols and sentries, he still could not keep his eyes off her. Gilded by moon and starlight, the mysterious Southern spy seemed to Houston the most extraordinary woman he had ever met. One infinitely more fascinating than the shallow Southern belles he had often consorted with in the past.

Candice was a truly remarkable woman. She was brave, resourceful, and tireless. Houston marveled at the way in which, time after time, Candice displayed her cool nerve and sharp wits as they managed to escape the grasp of the Union noose tightening on this part of Alabama. For example, just before sunset, at a stone bridge they needed to cross outside of some little hamlet, they'd been caught flat-footed by two Union soldiers with drawn guns. Candice had charmed the poor, unsuspecting Yanks to distraction, allowing Houston to get the drop on both men. Fortunately, he'd persuaded the soldiers to drop their weapons and leap off the bridge. And from the water, the ridiculous, smitten fools had *still* been so mesmerized by Candice's beauty that they'd blown her farewell kisses.

Houston chuckled at the memory of those lovesick blue-coats. Had he been alone, Houston figured there would have been bullets flying for certain and either he or that pair would be dead.

But Candice was such an enigma! Houston had never been with a woman for so many hours and still known

so little of her background. That, of course, would change.
He'd find out everything about her, given a little more time.
He would revel in the unraveling of her mysterious past.

"How much farther to Ashley?" he asked for perhaps the
tenth time.

Candice glanced sideways to regard him as if he were an
impatient boy. "I keep telling you, Houston, we'll be there
tonight."

"Then what? This Major Pritchard will most certainly
have fled along with the other Confederate troops. Either
that, or he'll have been shot or sent north by rail to a Union
prison."

Candice said nothing but Houston sensed the woman's
deep concern. "Listen," he said, "I didn't mean to sound so
pessimistic. It's just that I don't see any point in continuing
on to Ashley. Major Pritchard will have already fled this
part of the South. Besides, even if he were in Ashley,
whatever your message, I'm sure that it is irrelevant by
now, given how war changes things day by day."

"Some things never change," Candice said. "The major
must be in Ashley. What I have to tell him is for his ears
alone and it is of vital importance."

"But . . ."

"Houston, my dear man, I can never hope to repay you
for escorting me through so many dangers. You will always
be in my thoughts no matter what might happen. You're
one of the most brave, gallant, and honorable men I have
ever met."

"Not that honorable," Houston corrected. "And besides,
after we reach Ashley—and even if, by some miracle,
Major Pritchard is alive and we can deliver the message—
I am hoping we'll both return to Pineville, rejoin my family,
and that you'll continue on with us to the Indian Territory."

"That is impossible."

"But why? It's not going to be safe for you to remain in
this part of the South. You were exposed as a spy when
you and Mr. Farnum fled Chattanooga."

Candice merely smiled and rode on in silence. It was driving Houston wild.

"What if you are killed?" he asked. "God forbid, but what if we are fired upon and some fool shoots you instead of me? What then becomes of this message that is so damnably important to the South? Will it be lost?"

"I suppose it would be."

Houston saw a crack in her armor. He sensed that if he could gain her confidence he might win her heart. "But . . . but if you at least confided in me, then *I* could deliver it!"

Houston reached out and touched her on the arm. "Trust me. Open up and tell me what this is all about so that I can share your burden."

She laughed. Actually laughed! Houston withdrew his hand, feeling like a ninny. Here he was, a man who prided himself on being reserved, strong willed, and resolute in all matters, and she was scorning his offer of assistance as if it were nothing. Shamed, he lapsed into a morose silence.

"Tell me about your family," she said, after they had ridden for several more miles. "Like everyone else from Tennessee, I've heard of the famed Ballou horses and assume that these magnificent animals we are riding count themselves among that illustrious lineage of Thoroughbreds."

"They do," Houston admitted, realizing how childish it was to pout. "My father, killed by those who should have died to protect him, spent his entire life developing the bloodline. If I do say so myself, they are considered the equal of any racehorses in America. That's why we are so desperate to save these last few animals from the ravages of war."

"As well you should be! In a way, Houston, your charge is even more important than my own."

"Oh, I wouldn't go that far. You are trying to deliver a secret message that will no doubt save lives and perhaps even bring a few final, glorious victories to the South. My brother, sister, and I merely seek to save a line of extraordinary horses."

"What is the one you are riding called?"

"High Boy. His twin brother, the stallion that we left back at the wagon, is High Fire. He's got a little more red in his coat. When the sun hits it out in the paddock, it flames like he's on fire."

"They are beautiful horses," Candice smiled. "Houston, I suppose you were the one that would have taken your father's place at Wildwood."

Houston shrugged his shoulders. "Maybe. I'm the oldest living son now. So I guess I might still—if there's anything left to return to after the Yankee invaders march through on their way to Atlanta."

"There will always be the land," she told him. "You can rebuild. We'll all have to rebuild when this war is over."

"Yeah." He looked at her. "Wildwood Farm rests in one of the most beautiful parts of Tennessee. And for a lady like you, Chattanooga is just a few hours' buggy ride away. Perhaps . . ."

"Ashley," she interrupted, "is just ahead. I think it would be safer if we left the road and tied our horses in the trees, then continued on into town on foot."

Houston tried to hide his disappointment. "Yeah. Good idea. Do you know where to start looking?"

"Of course."

"Then lead the way, Miss Candice, whoever you are."

She did lead the way after they tied their horses in the forest. Houston, with a knife in his boot top, two pistols, and that Spencer Rifle he had taken from Lieutenant Pike before shooting the man in the neck, followed warily. There was enough moonlight to see that Ashley was not an especially large town. Certainly less than five thousand people could have lived here, given the number of houses and businesses.

Candice knew exactly where she wanted to go and she wasted no time. She brought them right out onto the main street and boldly strolled up a residential street lined with huge, two-storied mansions.

Houston was ashamed to admit that his heart was in his throat. He kept touching the butt of his six-gun, determined to sacrifice his own life, if necessary, to save Candice. Any moment he expected to be challenged by some Union guard but, as yet, he had not seen a single soldier. He decided that they were probably camped at the town square or city park. Ashley would be crawling with them come daybreak.

At the corner of streets named Baker and Taylor, Candice stopped so suddenly that Houston, who had been following a little behind, nearly crashed into her.

"What is it!"

"*Shhhh!* Listen!"

He listened.

"Someone is coming! It must be a patrol. Hurry, over here!" she whispered, grabbing his hand and yanking him off the walk and around behind a hedge, where they flattened on a lawn.

Houston pulled his hand free and dragged his Colt from its holster. Seeing him, Candice shook her head frantically, indicating that he was to holster the weapon.

Houston did as she wanted, but he wasn't happy about any of this, and when two Union soldiers sauntered past on the other side of the hedge, he made up his mind that, beautiful or not, he was going to have to reach a better understanding with this woman. One or the other of them had to be in charge, and it damn sure wasn't going to be a woman.

"This way," she whispered, jumping up to dash across the elm-lined street. Her grace and swiftness made it seem to Houston that Candice scarcely touched the ground, but instead, flowed across it like a wraith.

Houston shivered. He wanted to call this whole affair off right now, only she was motioning him to hurry up and follow.

"Blast!" he muttered. "She's going to get us both killed!"

But he followed. He ran across the street and grabbed her outstretched arm. "In here," she said.

Houston realized that they were standing on the doorstep of a very impressive mansion. One far more regal than their own home at Wildwood Farm, with porticoes and soaring spires. It was constructed of red brick and it reminded him of some of the mansions he'd once seen when boating along the Potomac on the yacht of a lady friend.

"Major Pritchard lives here?"

"Yes! Come along!"

He followed her up the stairs of a wide veranda and she amazed him once more when she reached into a pocket hidden inside of her shirt to produce a single house key. A moment later, they stepped inside. The foyer was immense. Moonlight glistened on marble columns and tiles. A chandelier so massive it could have illuminated a town hall hung overhead. Bronze sculptures competed with gilded portraits for Houston's rapt attention.

"This is . . ."

"Please," she whispered, "we mustn't wake the household staff or we are doomed. Be silent as a mouse and stay right behind me."

Houston glanced up at the portrait of an imperious figure dressed in an American Revolution uniform. Some long-forgotten general, no doubt, whose eyes seemed to warn him of danger. Houston swallowed and hurried after Candice on the tips of his toes. Down the marble hallway they crept, every squeak of their shoes seeming to announce their presence. They passed a door leading into a shadowy room that appeared to be an immense library, then slipped past another room that led off to a kitchen.

Candice stopped. She placed her hand on a doorknob. When she turned her lovely wrist, the knob squealed in modest protest, then the door opened and Candice fetched a match from the secret pocket and struck it on the wall.

For an instant, Houston was blind. Then, he saw that they were in a cavernous bedroom in whose center rested a gigantic four-poster bed in which a half dozen people could have slept without touching. He blinked and saw a walruslike man sit up quite suddenly. The man was very distinguished looking and he squinted and waved his hands before him as if he were trying to shoo away a swarm of fireflies.

"Who the . . ."

Candice shut the door, turned, and reached into the folds of her dress.

"Damn you to hell!" she cried, dropping the match as she pulled out a bowie knife. "Damn you in hell!"

The room was plunged back into darkness. Houston heard the man in the bed cry out in terror. This was a nightmare! Houston staggered forward in the darkness, mind reeling.

"*Ahhhh!*" A death scream—followed by the thud of hammered flesh.

"*Uggggh!*"

"Candice! Candice!"

Houston collided with a piece of furniture. A moment later, the room burst with light and his nightmare became reality for he saw that Candice had driven her knife deep into the man's chest.

"Dear God!" Houston said, gasping. "Candice, what have you done! Who are you!"

She turned on him, then lifted her riding skirt and found a two-shot derringer bound to her shapely leg by a red silk garter.

Houston took a step back. He believed he was going to die and his hand moved closer to the gun on his hip. He was prepared to fight for his life.

Once again he repeated, "Candice, who *are* you?"

"Who I am is not the right question."

"Then what is the 'right' question?"

"Who and why."

"All right, who was that man and why did you stab him to death?"

Candice took a deep breath. The derringer in her fist was rock steady. "I've just assassinated Mr. Kenyon J.

Armond, the wealthiest and most vile and treacherous man in Alabama."

Houston had heard of the man, but not in those terms. Armond was a prominent politician and philanthropist. He had also been very opposed to secession and had tried extremely hard to become the arbitrator of an agreement between the North and South that would have averted the war.

Kenyon J. Armond had failed, but not without gaining the respect of both Presidents Lincoln and Jefferson Davis. Houston knew that the man whose blood was still pumping from his body had been a Southern aristocrat in the truest sense and one of the most influential men in Alabama.

"Candice, tell me the truth, are you mad!"

Ignoring his question, Candice used the dying match to light the wick of a kerosene lamp. She turned the wick down very low.

"If I explain, will you really listen?"

Houston tore his eyes from the dead man. He wished Armond would close his eyes because he was staring directly at him. Houston moved a little off to the side. "I'll try."

"Kenyon was the main liaison for those of us sent north to spy for the South," Candice said, the derringer still trained on Houston's chest. "The mighty Kenyon Armond provided us names and arranged introductions at the very highest levels of President Lincoln's government and military cabinets in Washington, D.C. He saw to it that we were all well provided for at his own personal expense. Our job was to gain military secrets."

"But—"

"Let me finish," Candice demanded. "We *revered* this man until the day we finally realized—those of us who had not already been exposed, jailed or executed by the Union's intelligence corps—that dear old Mr. Kenyon Armond was really a *Union* sympathizer! He was in President Lincoln's camp."

"Have you any proof that what you say is true?"

"I hope to find it in this room."

Houston looked around. He spotted a crystal decanter and glasses on a bureau close by. Without asking permission, he went over and poured himself a stiff drink. He tossed it down, then poured another.

"Why don't you pour me one, too, like the gentleman that you are," Candice said. "Kenyon drank nothing but the finest. I could use a stiff drink."

"I'm sure that you could." Houston poured, and only when he handed the glass to Candice did he realize that the derringer was no longer clenched in her fist.

"What happened to Major Pritchard?"

"I made the name up. If I'd told you my real purpose was to assassinate Kenyon, you'd have tried to stop me."

Houston shook his head. "This is . . . is bizarre. That man was a national figure and, without proof of what you say . . ."

"Proof? The proof is resting in unmarked graves around Washington. The proof is in dead Southern spies betrayed by that monster!"

"Lower your voice! Remember, there are house servants."

"Damn them all," she said, tossing her bourbon down neat. "Kenyon was directly responsible for the deaths of no less than eight of the Confederacy's best spies. Not only that, but because we were being fed false and misleading information regarding Union battle plans and strategies, he could well be responsible for the deaths of *thousands* of our soldiers."

"I . . . I still need some proof!"

In reply, Candice flipped the derringer to Houston, who caught it with surprise. "What the . . . ?"

"Fire that derringer and they'll come running," Candice said. "Those Yankee guards that we ducked out beside the hedge, they are here to *protect* Kenyon. I wouldn't be surprised if there are more sleeping somewhere close by."

Houston wrapped his fingers around the derringer. "I don't know what to believe."

"The only thing that counts right now is what you intend to do next."

Candice poured herself another drink but did not bring it to her full lips. "Houston, it's very, very simple. You can either believe me and help me find whatever secret files Kenyon may have kept on the rest of us who have not yet been captured or shot—or disbelieve me and use that derringer. Those are your only two choices."

"I'm not going to shoot you!"

"Then help me search this room and this house. We must locate the man's secret files! Do that and you'll have your proof."

"If he was a secret master spy for the Union, why wouldn't he already have given the Southern spy list to Washington, D.C.?"

"Good question. Kenyon knew that information was power. If he just handed everything over to the Union generals, he'd diminish his own value. Much more intelligent to have that information his own private secret. That way, Kenyon remained inexpendable."

"I see," Houston said, nodding his head. "You're telling me that, in this spy business, no one trusts no one. Not even the people they report to."

"Exactly."

"I'm glad I'm just a simple horseman," Houston confessed.

"Dear Houston, there is nothing 'simple' about you. You are like most Southern gentlemen in that you take things as they are presented—at their word. I regret I've lost that trusting nature of yours, but I do so admire it."

"I feel . . . almost useless beside you."

Candice came up and slipped her arms around his neck. Her lips were warm, her breath sweet, and her body full and yielding. Houston drank her in like a rare, exotic wine that made his head spin and his heart skip like a child at play.

"If we survive this," he said, "will you stay with me?"

"Please," she whispered, "help me find those documents. There is so little time. Later, we can talk about later."

He nodded with reluctance, then placed his glass and the derringer on the bed. He walked over to stare at Kenyon Armond's corpulent body and the knife buried to the hilt in his chest.

"Houston?"

"All right," he sighed, turning to face her, "where do we begin?"

"We start in this room. Look for secret compartments in the walls. Or books that are hollowed out and might hold documents. Look at everything!"

At least one thing was now clear, Houston thought, Candice was in charge, not him.

THIRTEEN

"I think I've found it!" Candice said excitedly. "This must be the list!"

Houston moved swiftly across the library, where he'd already examined hundreds of books to see if they had hollow insides that contained the alleged secret list of Southern spies. He saw her holding a small piece of brown paper.

"Where was it?"

"Rolled up and inserted into this cigar," she said, shaking her head with amazement. "Look!"

Candice showed Houston how the thick Cuban cigar was really nothing more than a thin outer sheath of tobacco leaves. It had been cleverly hollowed out and a plug was inserted at one end so that no one would ever suspect it was fake.

"If the truth of Kenyon's past was ever discovered here," Candice explained, "he could simply have selected this cigar, lit it, and burned up the list without anyone realizing what he was doing."

"Brilliant."

"That he was," Candice said, her voice betraying her bitterness. "I remember the first time I came here for training before I was sent north. I remained . . . well, too long. And during all that time, I was in awe of the man. Kenyon was remarkable in so many ways."

Houston felt an unexpected pang of jealousy. Candice talked about the dead man as if she had almost worshiped him. As if she . . . she had even loved him.

"Houston, do you remember how I dropped the match and plunged his bedroom into darkness before I . . . I did what was necessary?"

"How could I ever forget?"

"I planned it that way. I knew that I could never kill him if I could see his face. Look into eyes that had always seemed to bore into my soul."

"Did he really have such an extraordinary influence over you?" Houston asked, not believing that any man could ever control such a woman.

"Yes," she admitted. "And not only me, but the others as well. Most were intimidated by him."

"He was a very powerful man in this state."

"His power," Candice said, "extended far beyond the boundaries of Alabama. You have no idea."

"Nor do I care." Houston was getting annoyed with all this talk about a dead Southern traitor. "May I see that list you found?"

"As proof I am not just some crazy murderess?"

"Yes," he said, feeling a little ashamed.

She unrolled the list. It was on a palm-sized leaf of fine parchment paper colored brown like a tobacco leaf. The names were printed in a very small hand, with black ink that could only be read when held up to the lamplight. How Candice discovered such a list was a mystery unto itself. Houston knew he could have searched for an eternity and never have found it.

Now Houston stared at the list. There were perhaps twenty or twenty-five names. At least half were neatly crossed out. Candice's name was not among them. Therefore, Houston realized with considerable dismay, the list was meaningless and proved nothing.

He looked up at her beautiful face with a question in his eyes. When Candice offered no explanation, he stammered, "But this is just a list of names."

"What did you expect? Perhaps a heading that read, 'Secret Southern Spies'?"

"No, of course not, but . . ."

"It's not 'just' names," she patiently explained, "it's the names of his spies, and the ones that are crossed out are dead."

"How do I know that?"

"Why else would he hide such a list?"

"Your *own* name isn't among them."

She took a deep breath and said, "That's because my name isn't Candice."

His jaw must have dropped because she reached out with a forefinger to press the point of his chin. "Now you're going to ask me what my real name is, and I can't tell you."

"But why?"

She looked down at the list and for a moment he saw that he had lost her. When she looked up again, it was to say, "I've memorized those people that have not been eliminated, and each of them must be warned. Now, I want you to keep the list."

"I don't want it!" He backed away, unsure if he could ever completely believe this woman.

"Please. We still have to get out of this town alive. If I were caught, I'd confess to murdering Kenyon. I'd say that you were tricked into bringing me here and played no part in the murder. With luck, they might even set you free. Then you could find a way to deliver this list to Jefferson Davis personally. They'd do the rest."

"Why can't I simply memorize the names, too?"

"You'd never be believed by the Confederacy on your word alone. But with this list, you could describe me and they'd know my real name."

He swallowed, wanting to kiss her mouth so bad he ached inside. "I'd describe you as the most beautiful, intriguing woman I've ever known. As the woman that I'd like to . . ."

"*Shhh,*" she whispered. "Please don't say anything more. We have to leave before daybreak. We are almost out of time!"

Houston twisted around to stare out the window. Sure enough, the night sky was fading. "Let's get out of here," he said, taking her hand and heading for the door.

In the hallway, they crashed into a house servant. The light was very poor but Houston knew the kitchen worker was a large woman. He was even more certain of that when she began to scream at the top of her lungs.

"Let's go!" Houston shouted, dashing for the front door with Candice in tow.

They skidded outside to see three Union soldiers sprinting across the street toward them. Rectangles of light were beginning to dot the front yard as the upstairs rooms of the mansion were illuminated by the startled household staff.

"The back door!" Candice shouted, pulling Houston back inside.

They raced the complete length of the marble hallway. Collided with another house servant and then finally reached the back door of the mansion.

A large dark shadow launched itself from the darkness and Houston's blood chilled as he heard the deep rumble of a massive dog. He drew his gun and fired. The dog kept coming, so he fired again and it yelped and began to roll.

"Come on!" he yelled.

They ran out under the trees hearing confused shouts from the house and then from the soldiers who were swarming in from other parts of town. They ran up the street, trying to stay in the shadows even as the darkness retreated before the rising sun.

"The horses are north of us!" Candice yelled. "We're going the wrong way!"

Houston was wild to get out of Ashley any way that he could. If only they could escape, they could always circle back through the forest and find their Thoroughbreds. And once they were mounted, nothing could catch them. They'd gallop back to Pineville and rejoin Ruff and Dixie.

"This way," he said, breaking from the sanctuary of a

stable and pulling Candice along behind as he streaked across a wide swath of open ground.

They were halfway across when six cavalrymen charged out from between buildings and quickly overtook them. Glancing over his shoulder, Houston could see that there was no way that they could reach the woods.

"Go!" he shouted, propelling her past him as he dragged pistols up from his holster and waistband. Houston took aim and would have died well except that Candice jabbed her derringer into his neck.

"Drop it!" she ordered. "Drop it or I will have to kill you!"

Houston began to turn around to stare at her to make sure that his mind was not playing tricks on him, but she shoved the derringer even deeper into his flesh. "Drop those pistols and don't move!"

"Candice," he whispered, dropping his pistols. "What . . . ?"

"Thank God!" she screamed as a handsome young lieutenant drew his horse up before them. "Lieutenant, this man has just robbed and murdered my dear husband!"

The lieutenant stared. Candice slipped the derringer into her dress pocket and threw herself into the startled Union officer's arms. "Oh thank God you arrived in time to save me!"

"Mrs. Armond?" the officer whispered when she stepped back and he could see her lovely face in the growing light. "Mrs. Armond, we thought you were in Washington, D.C., meeting with Mrs. Lincoln!"

Houston groaned. He had been duped and felt a crushing sense of doom. It was clear now that, in Candice, or whatever her name really was, he had finally met his match.

"I was," she said, "but I arrived by carriage late last night and then this . . . this monster killed my poor husband and . . ."

Candice broke down and wept pitiously, and Houston, with all those Union boys holding their damned Springfield

rifles trained on him, wished they'd just pull the trigger and
put him out of his misery and confusion.

Handcuffed and shackled at the ankles, Houston was led
under heavy guard into the room where a Major Anderson
and his staff sat beside Candice, draped in black and looking
devastated.

"Prisoner," the major said, standing up from his chair
behind a large table. "Do you admit to the robbery and
murder of Mr. Kenyon J. Armond?"

"Hell no!" He pointed at Candice. "*She* murdered him!
She's a spy!"

Candice's hand flew to her mouth and fresh tears erupted
from her eyes. No less than four officers rushed with their
handkerchiefs to attend to her, and it made Houston so
disgusted that he would have strangled the lovely, lying
creature if only it were possible.

"Why?" the major asked, his voice shaking with rage.
"Why did you murder one of your own best leaders! Mr.
Armond was the one man that might have been able to
help the South in the dark hours after its fall. Sir, do you
have any idea at all of what you have done to your fellow
countrymen?"

Houston squared his shoulders. In the hours since his
capture, he had debated whether or not he should tell his
captors about the spy list. If the list was a phony like
everything else concerning the woman, then presenting it
would not help him. And if it were a true list of Southern spies, then he would be selling his soul, probably for
nothing. And brave Southerners would die. And so, in a
moment filled with tortured doubts, he'd managed to pry
the list from his pocket and eat the damned thing.

"What is your real name, sir?"

Houston glared at them and said nothing.

"Very well. Mrs. Armond has raised the possibility that
you might have been sent here to gain some kind of diplo-
matic information."

"What?"

"That being the case," the major said, "I am going to send you north to Washington, D.C. There are people there who know how to get the truth out of you before you are sentenced and executed by a firing squad."

The major turned to Candice. "My staff and I have discussed your situation, Mrs. Armond, and there are some troubling inconsistencies in your story."

"*What* inconsistencies?"

"You didn't arrive late last night," he said, studying her face very closely. "No one can corroborate that."

"I arrived by carriage!"

"Then present your driver and the vehicle."

Candice paled. "I . . . I sent them back to Chattanooga."

"In the middle of the night? Why?"

Candice looked at the other officers seated behind the table. "I can't explain that here. But there are people in Washington who know my reasons."

"Perhaps there is someone right here in Ashley who can provide some insight into these troubling questions and inconsistencies."

"I don't know what you are talking about, Major Anderson, but you are treading on very thin ice. If my superiors hear of this . . . this inquest, you might well find yourself in a great deal of trouble."

"Oh?" The major smiled. "We'll see who is in trouble or not."

He made a signal to the guard at the door and a moment later, the door was opened.

"Robert!" Candice whispered.

Houston stared at the man that Ruff had whipped on the road for mistreating a team of carriage horses. Robert Farnum's broken nose was still badly swollen and there were dark circles around his eyes. It would take some time for the marks of his beating to disappear.

"Hello, my dear," Farnum said with a gloating smile. "Surprised to see me?"

Candice shook her head. "So, you've also betrayed us!"

"Of course. Only fools back a loser. And who else could have kept an eye on things in Washington for your late dear husband? Tsk, tsk, love, a knife in the chest? How barbaric! I expected better of you."

"You filthy swine! You . . ."

"Candice!" Houston's voice was loud and commanding. Now he firmly believed in this woman's true loyalty to the South and he wanted to protect her from rashly implicating herself. "I think we *both* had better say no more. Don't you agree?"

She blinked. Gathered her rattled composure. "Yes," she said, looking deep into Houston's eyes. "You are quite right."

Major Anderson was not pleased. "Mrs. Armond, I think it is obvious that you have been spying on behalf of the Confederacy."

"Prove it." Candice pointed a finger at Robert Farnum. "It is only his word against mine."

The major frowned. He studied his fingernails and then the other officers. Finally, he said, "There is no doubt in my mind, Mrs. Armond, that you are a dangerous Southern spy. You have betrayed my administration and murdered your own husband."

Anderson's voice hardened as he continued, "There is also little doubt in my mind that you will be executed after a federal court finds you guilty of those charges. Therefore, I will also send you north on the same train that will deliver your accomplice to the federal authorities."

"And am I also to be chained and shackled like a common murderer?"

"There is nothing even remotely 'common' about you, Mrs. Armond. And no, you will not be handcuffed or shackled. But you will be under guard."

"This is outrageous!"

The major shrugged. "Guards, remove these two from my sight and make sure they are on tomorrow's train."

And with that, Major Anderson got up and left the room.

• • •

Very early the next morning, Candice paid Houston a visit. She was flanked by a pair of very nervous guards that she had bribed. One said, "Two minutes, Mrs. Armond. That's all we can give you. And if we are caught . . ."

"Leave me to speak privately to this man," she demanded. "That was our agreement."

The guards left the room. Candice gripped the bars and Houston laid his hands on hers. "Houston, do you trust me now?"

"Yes. And love you."

At these words, her eyes misted. "I'll find a way to save us. I have friends in high places. You won't be tried for treason and executed."

"What about you?"

"I'll be fine."

Houston cleared his throat. "Forgive me for thinking you had betrayed me when we were arrested and then again in front of the major. I understand your motives now. You *had* to be the one that was above suspicion. It was the only way that you could have saved me."

"I . . . I'm sorry that it worked out like this. I was a fool not to realize that Robert had remained loyal to my husband. I've only learned in the last few hours that he murdered some poor blacksmith and that your brother is being sought for the crime."

"Ruff?"

"I'm afraid so."

Tears welled up in Candice's eyes. "Oh, dammit, Houston, everything has gone so wrong!"

"We'll find a way to make it right."

She drew herself up to her full height. "Yes, of course we will! I have to go now. But I had to let you know that there is hope."

"Time is up," one of the guards hissed, rushing inside. "Let's go, Mrs. Armond!"

Before she could be torn from his grasp, Houston clenched her hand. "I have to know something. What is your *real* name?"

"Molly. Molly O'Day."

"That's a beautiful name."

They would have kissed, but Molly was pulled back from the cell. Just before she disappeared, however, she turned her lovely face and Houston's spirits soared to see that Molly was smiling.

FOURTEEN

On the same morning that Houston's shackles were being inspected for the long journey north, Ruff and Dixie arrived on the outskirts of Ashley with their Thoroughbred horses. They could see puffs of smoke emitting from the stack of a locomotive and when they circled the town in an attempt to spot Houston, they stumbled across the two missing Thoroughbreds. It was a reunion of mixed emotions.

"These horses have been tied here for a long time," Ruff said, untying them.

"They're probably dying of thirst," Dixie said. "Let's return to that little stream that we passed back a ways."

"All right." Ruff studied the town. There was a lot of activity and the train depot was crawling with blue uniforms. "But I have a bad feeling about all of this. Houston would never leave horses to suffer this long."

"I tell you," Dixie said, taking the reins of the mare that Candice had ridden, "that woman will be the death of him."

Ruff led off back through the trees and they soon came upon the stream. He let all the animals drink their fill while he tried to figure out what to do next.

"If we just ride into town on these horses, we're going to attract a lot of attention from the Yanks," Dixie argued.

"I know that, but we must find out what happened to Houston. If he wasn't either dead or arrested, he'd have been back for the horses."

141

Dixie bit her lower lip and sat cross-legged on a bed of soft pine needles. "I don't think he's dead. I think he's just . . . just in trouble."

"What makes you think that?"

"He's slick," Dixie said. "He's a fighter, but he's also slippery with his tongue. My hunch is that he's talked his way out of getting himself killed."

Ruff was more than willing to believe his brother was still alive.

"He's a smooth talker, all right. Probably the smoothest of the bunch of us."

"He's the *only* one that is smooth," Dixie said. "All the rest of you men—Pa included—would rather act than talk."

"Never mind that," Ruff said, unwilling to be distracted from the real problem. "If he's been captured, how are we going to get him away from the Yanks?"

"If you're afraid that we'd attract too much attention by riding into Ashley," Dixie said, "then stay here with the horses and I'll go in on foot."

"I'm not letting you out of my sight."

"Why not?" Dixie demanded as she suddenly began to pull off her boots. "No one is going to arrest a bare-foot girl."

"Dixie . . ."

"I'm going, Rufus Ballou! Houston can be a pain, but he's also my brother and any fool can see that I've got the best chance of finding out what has become of him."

Dixie had that drop-dead look in her eye that said she was using her mule mind instead of her right mind. That meant he'd either have to hog-tie her or let her go.

"All right," he said, "but dammit, if you aren't back in an hour, then I'm coming after you."

"An hour and a half," she argued. "It'll take me most of an hour just to walk into town, scout around, and get back here without seeming to hurry."

"Dammit, not a minute longer! And you can't be wearing that six-gun strapped to your skinny hips."

"They're not any skinnier than yours."

"They're supposed to be wider."

Dixie pinned him with her hot black eyes. "Sometimes you say the dumbest things, Rufus. Sometimes you make me want to bang you right in the mouth."

Ruff backed down. "Listen, never mind all this," he said. "Just unbuckle the holster and gun and give them to me."

"Not a chance! I won't go in among those blue-coated beasts unarmed."

"Then here," Ruff said, extracting his father's pepperbox from his saddlebags. "Hide this but don't use it unless your life depends upon it."

Dixie took the pistol. "Sure is an old blunderbuss, isn't it," she observed with a frown. "And heavy, too. I told Pa a couple of times that he ought to get himself a good pistol instead of one of these old things that you can't hit the side of a barn with at arm's length."

"You're right about them being inaccurate," Ruff said, "but I never saw anything that would scare a man so bad as six barrels staring him in the face all at once. You ever seen a pepperbox misfire all its barrels?"

"No."

"It'll blow the head off a horse," Ruff said solemnly, "or cut down a fair-sized tree."

Dixie slipped the heavy pepperbox into the pocket of her riding habit. She frowned and had to pull the dress up a little. Next, she pitched her hat away and shook out her hair.

"Good," Ruff said with approval, "you look like a little tomboy—which you are."

"Drop dead," Dixie snapped.

She started to walk off toward Ashley, but Ruff grabbed her shoulder. Surprising both of them, he crushed Dixie to his chest and whispered, "You don't take any chances. You may be the only living Ballou besides myself. I'd not like to think of losing you, Dixie."

"Aw hell, Ruff," she said, pushing him away, "don't be talking foolish. I'm a girl! They're not going to bother me."

Ruff hoped she was right. She was still a girl. Skinny, but pretty enough that some women-starved soldier might take a shine to her. He shook his head, not even wanting to think about what could happen to Dixie if she were pawed and then taken advantage of by a bunch of soldiers.

"Here," he said, picking up a handful of dirt, walking over and smearing it on her arms, cheeks, and neck, "that will make it so you don't look so young, innocent, and pretty."

She grinned. "You think I'm pretty, Ruff?"

"Nope. Ugly as the south end of a mule."

Dixie's grin turned sour. "Well, so are you!" she cried. "And with that missing earlobe, you're a sight to make a girl run for the hills."

"I know that," he said, his voice softening. "Now, git! When you find Houston, just skedaddle back here as fast as you can and we'll both cook up a plan to get him loose." Dixie headed off through the woods toward Ashley. She had long, skinny legs and Ruff guessed that she'd cover the distance into town pretty damned quick.

At the edge of the woods, Dixie turned, and with her back shielding her hand, she gave Ruff a small wave. He waved back and that made Dixie feel a little braver, especially since she could see so many Union soldiers up ahead.

Dixie judged it took her less than five minutes to reach Ashley, where she mixed in with other civilians. No one paid her much attention and she listened to everything, hoping to hear something about Houston.

But all the talk was of the war. The citizens of Ashley were worried and afraid. Their town was being held by the Northerners and they feared that they would become victims of this war. Dixie learned that, indeed, General Bragg and his forces had been driven from Lookout Mountain in that final day of the Battle of Chattanooga.

From what Dixie was hearing among the townspeople, it was pretty well agreed that nothing could stop the Union armies from marching unopposed through the South. It was all that General Robert E. Lee and the remnants of his demoralized and battered Confederate army could do to keep from being trapped and annihilated. The mood in Ashley was black and on every Southern face, Dixie saw fear and despair.

"Houston!" She dropped her voice to a whisper and clapped her hands together with joy. "Houston."

He was being led from the town courthouse under a very heavy guard. Dixie's heart almost broke to see the way her brother was chained and shackled hand and foot. He looked neither to the left nor to the right as he was led toward the train depot.

Dixie cast caution aside. She rushed across the street so that she would be directly in the path of her brother.

"Out of the way, girl!" a corporal barked. "Can't you see we've got a prisoner!"

"Oh, I can see that just fine!" Dixie said in a loud, angry voice that brought smiles to the crowd of Southerners. "And I hope that he gets free and kills you all!"

The corporal swore and actually took a swing at Dixie, but she easily jumped out of his reach, yelling, "God protect you, mister!"

Houston's eyes had been locked on the street but now they jerked up to see Dixie. She winked at him, and Houston, bless him, was cheered by her rallying call and grinned broadly.

"Well, thank you, little lady! And don't you worry—there's not enough guards in the Union army to take me to Washington."

In reprisal, Houston was hammered between the shoulder blades with the butt of a Union rifle. It was all Dixie could do not to tear her father's pepperbox out from her dress and blow the offending guard's head from his narrow shoulders.

Dixie, like many of the sullen and half-rebellious citizens of Ashley, followed the cadre of guards and their prisoner down to the train depot. She knew that she ought to be racing back to get Ruff so they could figure out how to save Houston, but she could not bear to leave until Houston was out of her sight. And just before he was shoved onto the train, Houston threw a guard's hand off and looked down, eyes searching for his sister.

Dixie would never forget that moment. Unbowed, Houston raised his shackled hands and clenched his fists overhead. "Hurrah for Dixie!"

Dixie almost burst with pride as the startled crowd gaped, then erupted into cheers of admiration and support for Houston. Then, her brother was slammed through the doorway of the train and lost from her view.

Dixie realized that she was crying. She dried her eyes on her sleeves, then turned to rush back to the woods and get Ruff. Because of the tears, she didn't see Candice until she almost collided with that treacherous viper whom she blamed entirely for her brother's arrest.

"Out of the way!" shouted one of the Union soldiers who held Candice by either arm. "Out of the damned way!"

Dixie blinked her vision clear. With a start, she realized that Candice was being escorted by a military guard to the same train. She wasn't handcuffed or manacled like Houston, but she was definitely not free, either.

When Dixie pushed in closer, confused and unsure of what to say, Candice looked through her as though she did not exist and then she was moving past and being helped up onto the train.

Dixie stared in confusion. Surely Candice had recognized and remembered her. But the self-proclaimed Southern spy had shown no evidence of recognition. That made Dixie wonder if she had misjudged the woman from the very start and she really had been working against the North.

There was no time to be wrestling with so many unanswered questions, so Dixie whirled and hurried away, trying her very best not to break into a run that would carry her to Ruff's side before the train left for the North.

She returned to her brother and Ruff's expression grew bleak as he learned about his brother's predicament. "Getting Houston off that train isn't going to be easy. Did you see any civilians boarding?"

Dixie had to think about that for a few minutes. "No," she finally said. "Just soldiers. It's an army train but . . . well, I think I did see a few civilians."

"They probably work for the railroad," Ruff said, sighing. "I'm not sure which branch of the railroad this is, or even where it goes."

"Well, we can't just sit here and wait for it to leave!"

"I know that," Ruff snapped. "So . . . so maybe we ought to get a head start on the train."

"A head start?"

"Sure!" Ruff began to pace back and forth. "We have to stay with that train, either ahead or behind. Better ahead. We can follow the tracks."

"But . . ."

"There's no other alternatives right now," Ruff decided out loud as he strode over to High Man and tightened his cinch. "If that train gets away from us, Houston and Candice are goners. We'll never be able to help them once they cross the Mason-Dixon line!"

Dixie wasn't about to risk her life or that of her brothers to save Candice, but this didn't seem the time or the place to get into an argument, so she said, "What about the mares? They could never keep ahead of a train. Not in foal and for more than a few miles."

"I know."

"I won't leave them behind for them damned Billy Yanks!"

Ruff's mind raced. "We've passed several farms just outside of town. We could take our mares to one of them and pay the owner to keep them until we can return with Houston. It won't take long. A few days. I'll relay between High Man and one of the young stallions. You can ride the other."

"All right, but whoever takes our mares will have to hide them inside a barn. I'll be damned if I'll let some Union cavalry patrol take them, too!"

"That suits me right down to the ground," Ruff said, dropping his stirrup and then hurrying to untie the mares. "Let's go."

They were galloping out of the woods in minutes and heading east. Two miles away, they saw a farm that had a large barn, neat fences, and a nice house.

Ruff was satisfied. "I like the looks of this one."

"It isn't Wildwood but maybe it'll do," Dixie conceded.

"Then let's give it a try. For all I know, the train has already left Ashley."

They galloped right into the farmyard and it brought a pack of dogs surging out from under the porch. On their heels were several children, and then a young man and his wife appeared. Ruff did not waste any words. In a few terse sentences, he explained that they were in trouble and had to save their brother, who was on his way to a federal prison.

"I need you to hide our Thoroughbred mares from the Yanks until we return." He pulled out a wad of Yankee greenbacks that he'd gotten for their furniture, mules, and wagon. "I'll give you fifty Yankee dollars."

"Give him a hundred," Dixie said. "If we lose those mares, Pa's dream is dead."

Ruff looked back to the startled man. "Fifty now, fifty more Yankee dollars when we get the horses back. Agreed?"

The young farmer, Wade Calder, looked to his wife, Annie. She nodded vigorously. "All right," he said, taking the money, "but if the Yanks come and I can't keep them from going into that barn and taking your horses, then I'm not responsible. I won't die to stop them, not for a hundred or even a thousand dollars."

"Fair enough." Not willing to waste a minute, Ruff touched his heels to High Man's flanks and led the mares over to the barn. They were run inside and quickly placed in stalls. A glance around the interior told Ruff that his horses would be well cared for.

"Let's get your saddle on the stallion Houston was riding," Ruff said.

Dixie was already in motion, and within two minutes, they were back in the saddle and galloping to intercept the rails. The Thoroughbreds ran like the wind and soon they saw the railroad tracks that would carry Houston north.

Ruff reached down and touched the smooth, undulating shoulder muscles of his Thoroughbred. "We can do it," he vowed, leaning forward to coax and speak to the animal. "We can do it, High Man!"

The horse's ears were laid back and it ran on and on. When they intercepted the rails, Ruff twisted around in his saddle. He looked back to see a plume of smoke chasing them. Ruff pulled the great Ballou stallion down to an easy gallop. Better than any man alive, he knew that if they were going to race the iron horse, their horses were in for the longest, hardest race of their lives.

FIFTEEN

Ruff was sure of only one thing: he had to free Houston within twenty-four hours. After that, their Thoroughbreds would be too weary to keep pace with the Washington-bound train. They were already down in weight and strength. Making matters even more difficult was the fact that Ruff did not know which towns the train would stop at to take on coal or water.

"They've got to stop for the night," Dixie said as dusk was falling.

"Why?"

"Because there are so many Union officers on that train and there are only three passenger cars—none of them sleepers or diners."

"I hope you're right. I think our only chance of freeing Houston is at night. Hopefully, they'll stop at the next town."

"And if they don't?"

"We'll try and keep ahead of them tonight and see what tomorrow brings."

"It'll be the ruin of these stallions if we don't stop and let them eat and rest by tomorrow."

Ruff knew his sister was right. He had been relaying between High Man and one of his sons, but still, this grueling pace was taking a tremendous toll on their horses. High Man's years were beginning to tell and the old stallion was showing signs of great weariness.

"We'll give them some grain first chance."

"We're about out of that, too."

"I know," Ruff said. "I know."

Just after sunset, they galloped into a fair-sized town called Austin, and when they found its only livery, Ruff dismounted and went inside to talk to the owner. He reappeared a few minutes later with a short, barrel-chested man in his early fifties who wore bib overalls and held a pitchfork.

"Dixie, this is Mr. Rowe. He owns the livery and will take care of our stallions."

"I don't normally allow 'em on the property," Rowe said, "but your brother says they're all pretty mannerly."

"They are," Dixie said, "and they're so exhausted I'm sure they'll be very quiet."

Rowe studied the Thoroughbreds. "They're beauties, but they been hard used."

"No help for it," Ruff said apologetically. "We've never had to use horses so hard. It pains and shames us."

"Well," Rowe said, "sometimes a person gets in a fix and has no choice. Grain 'em, rest and brush 'em a mite, and they'll be fit as a fiddle in a few days."

"I'm afraid we don't have that long, Mr. Rowe," Ruff said. "We'll probably have to be on the run before daybreak."

The liveryman scowled. "Sounds like you're in trouble."

"The whole South is in trouble," Ruff replied, not wanting to say anything more than was necessary.

He turned to Dixie. "Mr. Rowe says that the train will spend the night here. If the visit holds to pattern, the officers and prisoners will be put up in that two-story brick hotel down the street."

The approach of the Union train was heralded by the loud wail of its steam whistle. "We'd best get these horses inside," Ruff said.

They left a few minutes later. As they neared the hotel, Dixie said, "I hope it has a fire escape or some way for us to reach Houston after they get him inside."

"Why wait until they're inside?" Ruff asked. "Why not go in first?"

That made sense to Dixie. She could hear the locomotive's shrill blasts growing louder and louder. "Look! Here comes the train!"

Sure enough, it was pulling into Austin, steam pouring out from its stack as it eased up to a water tower. About ten soldiers hurried to meet the arrivals, and Ruff figured it was now or never as far as his chances went of getting into the hotel.

The hotel didn't have a fire escape. Only a rear door, which was locked. "We'll have to go in the front door," he said grimly. "There's no other way."

For once, they were in luck. Just as they were about to enter the hotel, they saw the desk clerk step outside and hurry toward the train, leaving the lobby unattended.

"Let's go!" Ruff grabbed Dixie's hand and hurried through the front door and across the lobby. He paused only a moment at the registration desk, then his long arm shot out and he snatched the key for room 24 from its hook before they made a beeline for the stairs.

"Where are we going?" Dixie whispered as they hurried up to the second-floor landing.

"Room twenty-four," Ruff said, glancing at the key.

"But . . ."

"*Shhh!*" Ruff said. "We're just going to have to take our chances and hope for the best."

When they came to the room, they quickly opened it and went inside. It was small, but neat, clean, and unoccupied. Ruff hurried over to the window and stayed hidden behind the curtains as he watched the Union officers and guards escort Houston and Candice from the train. The Union soldiers moved rapidly from the train depot toward the hotel. Ruff and Dixie both watched until they disappeared below.

"The clerk is going to see that this room key is missing," Dixie said. "What will happen then?"

"I'm not sure," Ruff admitted, his mind racing. He drew both his six-guns and checked to make sure that they were primed and ready. "Dixie, are you still carrying Pa's pepperbox?"

"I lost it," she confessed. "I don't know when, but I did."

"Here, take this extra Colt of mine."

"Are we going to open fire if someone comes through that door?"

"Not unless we have to," Ruff said. "Besides, there's a chance that, since the key is missing, they won't use this room and we can find Houston later tonight."

"There are more Yanks than empty rooms," Dixie pointed out. "They'll need to use this room. And even if they didn't, how are we supposed to find Houston?"

"You're asking too many damned questions!"

"Well someone better ask them, because we need answers before they come up here!"

Ruff expelled a deep breath. "We need a place to hide."

"That'll be a neat trick," Dixie said, looking around the sparsely furnished room that did not even have a closet. "Where?"

"Only one place I can see."

Dixie followed her brother's eyes. "Under the bed? They'll see us for sure!"

Ruff had to admit that she was probably right. The bedspread was too small to reach the floor and there was no way to drag it down any lower on all sides. "You got any better ideas?"

"Yeah, if someone steps inside, you brain him."

"But what if there are several men?"

"Then I help."

"Okay." Ruff reversed his grip on the pistol. "Dixie, it'd be better if you distracted them."

"I can knock one out."

Ruff shook his head. "I'd rather you sat out in the open. It'll distract them long enough for me to hit 'em a good whack."

Dixie's expression told Ruff that she did not at all care for his plan, but with the sound of heavy footsteps pounding up the stairs, there was no time to argue, so she walked over to the bed and flopped down with her back against the headboard and her pistol resting in her lap.

Ruff stepped in behind the door and removed his hat. He heard loud voices in the hallway and then doors opening and closing up and down the hall. He was just starting to think that this room might not be used when he heard the metallic sound of a key entering their lock. It didn't take a lot of guesswork to decide that the desk clerk must have found a spare key. The door bumped open and Ruff raised his pistol overhead, his heart hammering against his sore ribs.

"Sergeant," the man behind the door said, "we'll have supper together along with Sergeant Grannis and Lieutenant Turner in one hour. I'll meet you downstairs in the lobby."

"We'll be ready, Captain," the sergeant replied. "And don't worry about the prisoner. I just wish that I was the one that was guarding Mrs. Armond tonight!"

The officer in the doorway of room 24 laughed, and so did several others in the hallway. Then the captain stepped into the dim room and closed the door behind him. He started for the bedside lamp, then saw Dixie.

"Who are . . ."

Ruff slipped up behind the Union officer and the butt of his Colt chopped downward. Ruff didn't want to kill the man, but he could not risk only partially stunning him so that the captain could shout with alarm. So the blow was plenty hard and the Union officer dropped as if he'd been brain-shot.

"What are we going to do with him?" Dixie whispered, jumping off the bed.

"Tear up some sheets. We'll gag and truss him up tighter than a fat lady in a corset."

Dixie ripped an entire sheet into strips and Ruff used them to tie the officer. The unconscious man was in his late thirties, plump and pleasant looking with mutton-chop whiskers and a bald spot on the back of his head, where an enormous goose egg was already developing.

"All right," Ruff said.

"All right, what?"

Ruff went over and lit the kerosene lamp. "All right, I don't know," he admitted.

"You don't know?"

"That's right." Ruff began to pace back and forth. "I don't know. Maybe the only thing we can do is just to start knocking on doors once we think most of the soldiers have gone to supper. I doubt they'll risk taking Houston. More likely they'll bring him back some food."

"I doubt they'll be that charitable," Dixie said. "But I guess your plan is better than nothing."

"Thanks for your overwhelming vote of confidence."

"I'm sorry," Dixie said. "It's just that there must be twenty or thirty rooms up here. The chance of finding the right one before we are discovered is not very good."

"We're all out of choices," Ruff said. "So we'll wait an hour to give everyone time to go and eat, then we search out Houston."

"Have you forgotten about Sergeant Grannis? When his captain doesn't show up in the lobby in one hour, he'll come looking for him."

Ruff strode over to the window. There was a short drop to the roof of the porch. "As soon as it's completely dark," he said, "we'll lower the captain through the window and drop him to the roof of the porch. No one will see him until tomorrow morning."

"He might break his neck if he lands on his head."

"A soldier's life is full of unforeseen dangers, Dixie. Better a broken neck than what we'll face if they catch us."

Dixie agreed and a short time later, they managed to lower the unconscious officer out the window. Thanks to Ruff's long, muscular arms, they were able to dangle the

Union captain within a few feet of the porch roof before dropping him.

"I didn't hear his neck crack," Dixie said, "but he sure is going to have a terrible headache tomorrow morning."

"That's his problem," Ruff said, heading for the door, "we've got a bunch of our own."

Without a better plan, they began to knock on the doors. The first rooms were empty but the fifth door brought a call. "Who goes there?"

Ruff's mind froze.

"Tell him Lieutenant Butler!" Dixie prompted in a whispered voice.

"Lieutenant Butler!"

"Just a minute, sir."

Ruff drew a second pistol from his waistband and glanced down to see that Dixie was also ready to start shooting.

The door opened a crack and Ruff threw his shoulder into it hard. The guard cursed and staggered back, and before he or the other two guards could recover, Ruff and Dixie had their guns up and cocked.

"What the . . . ?"

"Untie him!" Ruff commanded as he glanced at Houston. "And if any of you make a sound, so help me, it will be your last! No dead heroes!"

The guards had no intention of being dead anythings. Houston was quickly untied. "You two are something special," he said as he helped them tie and gag the Union guards. "I'd hoped for a miracle and you've answered my prayers."

"We've three stallions at the town livery," Ruff said. "We'll be out of here in no time at all."

But Houston shook his head. "Uh-uh."

"What the hell is that supposed to mean?"

"It means that I'm not going anywhere without Mrs. Armond."

Ruff's jaw dropped in amazement and Dixie cried, "That's crazy! You'll get us all killed."

"Then go wait for me at the livery," Houston ordered, "because I'm going to save the woman I love."

"What room is she in?"

"I have no idea," Houston admitted, "but it won't take me long to find her."

Ruff looked to his sister and said, "Dixie, I think we ought to stick together. What happens to one of us happens to all of us."

"I agree," she said before turning to Houston and saying, "Let's find her and get out of here fast."

"No shooting," Ruff warned. "If there are shots, we're finished, because there's no second-story fire escape and it's a long drop to the ground. One of us would probably break an ankle."

"So the only way out is down the stairs?" Houston asked.

"That's right."

Houston shook his head and muttered, "That's going to be a neat trick. The lobby is probably crowded with soldiers, any one of whom will recognize me."

"And they'll recognize you in that hallway," Dixie said. "So why don't you both stay here until I find Candice's room?"

"Molly," Houston corrected. "Her real name is Molly O'Day."

"Whatever," Dixie said. "When I find her room, I'll tell her guards that I've come up with a message or some such thing. It'll get the door open and then I'll pull a gun on them. We can see what happens from there."

"We'll be ready to help," Ruff promised.

"Count on it," Houston added.

"Then I'm going," Dixie said, checking her six-gun and making sure it was hidden in the folds of her dress before stepping into the hallway.

Dixie was scared half-witless when she began to work her way down the hall knocking on rooms. Twice, doors opened and she had to stammer that she was looking to deliver a message to Lieutenant Butler. The second time, a soldier with whiskey on his breath tried to drag her inside.

"You can give me a message, pretty little girl!"

Dixie didn't want to use her Colt unless it was absolutely necessary, so she raked the beast's cheek with her fingernails and managed to tear free.

"Damn you!" the soldier swore, taking a step outside of his room before turning to see Ruff's big fist coming into his eye.

Dixie was trembling badly but continued up the hallway until finally, a guard opened the door and she saw Molly O'Day sitting at a table with two other soldiers. When Molly saw her, the woman's eyes widened with surprise and Dixie looked back at the soldier who faced her.

"I have a message from Lieutenant Butler," she said. "It's for the lady."

"What is it?"

"I have to tell her personally."

The guard smirked. "A message, huh? Yeah, and I'll bet it has nothing to do with the army."

The other guards came over and one of them leaned against the doorjamb. "How old are you, pretty girl?"

"Fourteen."

"That's old enough for . . ."

The soldier's words died in his throat as Dixie's gun came up and stuck him in the gullet. His eyes widened and any thoughts he had of tearing the gun from Dixie's hand were forgotten when Ruff and Houston barged into the room. Fists flew and soldiers crashed unconscious to the floor.

Houston hurried over to Molly. "Let's get out of here!"

She threw herself into his arms, and Ruff waited as the pair held each other. Then he said, "We still have that one little problem, brother."

Houston nodded and, with his arm still around Molly, said, "We'd never make it down the stairs and across the lobby. Gather the sheets off this bed. Tear 'em into strips and tie them together. We'll lower ourselves out a back window into the alley."

Ruff and Dixie went right to work because Houston's plan was their only hope. It took no time at all to make a linen rope and feed it out the window.

"I'll go first," Ruff said, "and when I'm down and I know it's safe, I'll give a sharp pull."

They nodded. Ruff noticed that Houston and Molly were still holding each other tight, and even though they weren't saying much, they were saying a lot, if that made any sense. They were mostly just staring at each other, but the look in their eyes filled Ruff with envy. No woman had ever looked at him that way, and with his missing earlobe, it was unlikely now that one ever would.

The linen rope held Ruff's weight and the alley was deserted so he tugged. Dixie came down right behind him, followed by Molly. Houston was the last one out, and when they were all crouched in the alley, they hurried to the livery.

"Back so soon?" Rowe asked with surprise.

"Yeah," Ruff said, "we're on the run."

Rowe studied Houston and Molly. "Yeah, I seen them two being escorted off the train under armed guard. I guess you would be in a hell of a hurry."

Little was said during the next five minutes as the stallions were saddled and bridled. The Thoroughbreds hadn't had much time to rest, but they had all been grained heavily.

"They'll carry you a few more miles," Rowe said, leading a fine-looking mare out from another stall. "And this mare is for Mrs. Armond."

Molly was very grateful. "I'm sorry I can never repay you."

"Just helping a lady like you is payment enough, ma'am. Word is that you were a spy for Jeff Davis hisself."

Molly neither confirmed nor denied the statements.

"Yeah," Rowe said, "you couldn't admit that. I understand. Well, you just take this fine mare and give these damn Yankees a merry chase on her!"

"I will, sir. You can count on it."

"Come on!" Ruff said impatiently. "Let's ride. Someone is bound to sound the alarm any minute now."

But Houston wasn't listening. Not to Ruff. He was listening to Molly, and what she was saying made his heart want to break. "You've got to save your Thoroughbreds. I've got to save my friends in Washington."

"But . . ."

Molly touched his lips. "Please. I couldn't possibly do anything but return to Washington."

"But they'll be looking for you!"

"I know that. But I have friends that will help. And more to save. Good-bye, my love."

Houston protested. "I'll come with you. I'll . . ."

"You can't go where I have to go," Molly said, slipping her arms around his neck. "Our chances would be slim and none if we were together. Alone, I can do the things I must to save my friends."

Houston, the man who had broken so many hearts, made a small anguished sound. "Will I ever see you again?"

"I hope so. Someday. When this war is over."

"We're going to live among the Cherokee," Houston blurted. "And then maybe go to Texas. Or come back to Tennessee after the war. Molly, I hardly know you and yet . . . yet . . ."

Molly placed her finger over his lips to silence him. "I grew up in Memphis and once saw you and your family win a big horse race on the Fourth of July."

Molly pointed at High Man. "It was *that* horse that won the race. I was only thirteen and I'll never forget the way he ran that day."

The anguish left Houston's face. "Who was riding him?"

"You were," she said. "Houston Augustus Ballou. I never forgot the horse, or the name or the face."

"I was just a boy then."

"And I a young, impressionable girl. Good-bye, Houston."

He crushed her in his arms. "I love you, Molly! If you don't come West to find us, I'll return to find you!"

"Listen," she said urgently, "Robert Farnum can't let either of us alone now."

"But . . ."

"You have to believe I know what I'm talking about! He'll come after me—then you. We are the only two left who know the names on that secret list of spies. You *must* be vigilant!"

"If he harms you," Houston vowed, "he'll wish he'd never been born. I'll track him down to the ends of the earth."

"I hope that will never be necessary," Molly whispered. "But no matter what happens, just be careful, because Robert is a very dangerous and cunning man."

Houston tried to speak but failed, as her lips touched his own. Close by, Ruff had to look away.

"Let's go," Ruff said to his kid sister.

When they rode outside, Molly was gone and Houston's handsome face was wet with tears.

As he rode past, Ruff reached out and touched his brother's arm, and Dixie silently did the same. Then, they lined out west toward Ashley and their mares. At the edge of town, Ruff reined his horse, hearing the shouts of soldiers.

"They found those guards we tied and gagged," Dixie said solemnly.

"Yeah," Houston said, his voice heavy with indifference. "Let's ride on."

Ruff set the pace. He wished he could say something that would make his brother feel better, but he was not a man with the gift of words, so he just sat up straight in his saddle, paid attention to High Man, and rode the way he'd been taught by his father—like a horseman.

SIXTEEN

The Ballous rode that entire night in silence. At mid-morning the following day, they arrived at the Calder farm where they had left their mares.

"Here's the extra fifty dollars I promised," Ruff said, extending the money toward Wade Calder.

Surprisingly, Calder shook his head. "No, sir," he said, "me and the wife have been talking. This war is killing the South, and neither of us want to take such a profit from the misfortunes of our brothers in arms. You already paid us fifty dollars, and that's more than fair."

"Well, thank you," Ruff said. "We sold everything we owned including a fine pair of mules and a good wagon. Had to practically give them away. What money we have left, we'll need to start over again bulding a horse farm."

"Where are you people from?"

When Ruff told the young farmer, he shook his head solemnly. "I'm sorry to hear that."

"Why?"

Calder scratched the toe of his boot in the dirt and said, "I'm afraid that General Sherman and his army have already marched through your part of Tennessee and, from what I've heard, they've burned everything to the ground. Even the orchards and fences. They say their damned Yankee soldiers are worse than locusts going through a grain field. They kill anything that moves and eat everything that will bleed, squawk, bark, chew grass, or howl."

Ruff turned away. Up to now, he and Dixie had avoided the issue of Wildwood Farm. But both of them had secretly been hoping that their beloved horse ranch and fine mansion might have been spared. Now, like so many others since this war had begun, that hope was dashed.

"What about you, Mr. Calder?" Houston asked quietly.

"What about me?"

"Yes. And your family. Handsome woman and two beautiful children. Are you going to stay and wait for the Union army to come marching through?"

"Well . . . ," the young farmer said, shifting uncomfortably under Houston's hard gaze, "as a matter of fact, we was figuring to stay and take our chances. Maybe appeal to their better natures."

"Don't be a goddamn fool," Houston said in a voice suddenly gone hard. "Haven't you heard what is happening on the battlefields! Wounded men on both sides being bayoneted while they beg for mercy. Soldiers deserting to roam in gangs and pillage towns and farms. Rape. Murder and savagery."

Houston leaned forward in his saddle and jabbed a finger at the farmer, who stood wide-eyed in shock. "Mr. Calder, all those atrocities are commonplace. Get out of this country before the Union army destroys you and the entire South!"

The farmer glanced back at his house to see his wife and children standing in the doorway. They'd heard Houston and had been shaken by his tirade.

The farmer hitched up his overalls. He dragged a red bandanna out from his back pocket and, though the air was cool, mopped his brow. "You . . . you got no right to scare my woman and children, mister!"

Houston leaned back in his saddle. "And you've no right to be such a fool as to leave them at the mercy of Union soldiers."

"Easy," Ruff said to his brother, who looked so incensed that he might leap from his horse and actually attack the farmer. "Easy."

Houston's eyes slitted. "A man finds a good woman, he'd damn sure better learn to take care of her and the children he fathers."

The farmer retreated toward the house. "Your mares are in my barn," he called when he got back to the door, and then crowded his wife and two children into the little house. "You folks take 'em and git off my property! Hear me?"

"Yeah," Ruff said, reining High Man around and leading the way to the barn. In a few minutes, they had the Thoroughbred mares haltered and attached to lead lines.

"You didn't need to talk so hard to him," Dixie said as they rode out of the barn. The farmer was still in his doorway, except now he was alone and armed with a rifle. "You shouldn't have talked that way to him, Houston!"

"Oh, yes, I should have," Houston muttered. "The man is a fool. The Yankee soldiers will steal his stock, use his wife, and probably kill him if he interferes. Think what that will do to the mental state of his poor children."

Dixie twisted around in her saddle and studied the farmer for a long time. Then she raised her hand and waved when his wife and children reappeared.

None of them waved back.

Aunt Maybelle's plantation was tucked up against the base of Woodall Mountain, in the very northeastern corner of Mississippi. For many years, it had been a cotton plantation run by Ruff's uncle Sidney, but then Sidney had died and Aunt Maybelle, never having had children of her own, had decided to raise tobacco and truck crops instead. Most of what she produced was shipped to Memphis or Huntsville. Over the years, Aunt Maybelle proved to be a much shrewder businessperson than her late husband. Since poor Uncle Sidney's death, the plantation had prospered.

"I hope that the Yankees haven't burned her out same as us," Ruff said as they neared the plantation. "I'm not sure but what all the towns in these parts are now in Yankee hands."

"Aunt Maybelle will probably find a way to profit off the Yankees," Dixie said in sarcasm. "I never seen such a scheming, tight-fisted woman all the time claiming to be just a poor little old Southern lady."

"Dixie!" Ruff scolded. "Now, you can't be staying at her place thinking that."

"Fine, then take me with you to the Cherokee."

"We promised Pa we'd do it this way," Houston said. "And a promise is a promise."

"You had no right to make Pa a promise that *I'm* supposed to keep!"

"It was his dying wish!" Houston exploded. "What else do you expect? That we ignore it?"

Dixie clamped her mouth shut. She knew that it was hopeless to try and talk her brothers out of leaving her with Aunt Maybelle. The matter was closed. She would simply have to try and endure a month with the sanctimonious little fraud. Dixie figured she could stand anyone a month, even her aunt.

The road crossed a low rise of ground, where they reined in their horses. "There it is," Ruff said. "Looks just like it did the last time I saw it. Either the Union army missed it or Aunt Maybelle sweet-talked them into leaving her in peace."

When there was no comment on his observation, Ruff glanced at both Dixie and Houston. They appeared morose, and neither one seemed the least bit happy or excited to finally arrive at a place where one could sleep in a real bed, rest the horses, or generally take things easy after nearly a week of dodging Union patrols and riding mostly at night to keep from being captured.

Ruff guessed he should have expected that sort of reaction. Houston was still heartbroken and Dixie . . . well, Dixie was just plain furious that she'd have to stay behind.

"One of us ought to go down alone just in case," Ruff said. "Houston, you were always Aunt Maybelle's favorite. Why don't you go?"

"Might as well," he said lackadaisically. "If there's Union soldiers waiting down there in ambush, better I die than either of you."

Ruff started to say something angry but changed and watched Houston ride on down to Aunt Maybelle's plantation. His brother didn't even look good on a horse these days, all slumped over like a sack of grain.

"Boy, Dixie, I sure hope he pulls out of this soon. I never seen him so low in spirits. That Molly O'Day just broke his poor heart."

"He'll recover."

Her remark annoyed Ruff, who had been expecting a kinder answer. "You don't have much sympathy for him, do you."

"No. Not after all the ladies' hearts he's broken. Maybe now Houston will be a little kinder with the women whose heads he turns."

"Maybe."

Ruff remembered that his father had once told him that getting one's heart broken was like taking a dose of caster oil. It was all-fired bitter, but it was good medicine just the same. It made a good person kinder toward the opposite sex. It also gave handsome men and beautiful women some badly needed humility. So maybe it was a good thing for Houston, though it was painful to witness.

It took Houston a good quarter of an hour to reach Aunt Maybelle's yard. When he did, Ruff saw him dismount and then he saw Aunt Maybelle appear on her veranda. The woman's cry of joy could be heard clear up to where he and Dixie were waiting.

"Aunt Maybelle may have lost her husband," Dixie said, "but she hasn't lost her loud voice."

"I sure hope you don't talk like that around her. You'll hurt her feelings and just make everyone miserable."

"Her feelings?" Dixie repeated. "Ha! Aunt Maybelle isn't the sensitive type."

They watched Houston dismount, hug his aunt, then turn and motion them to come on along.

"Let's go," Ruff said, annoyed at the pained expression on Dixie's face. "It isn't the gallows."

"It's worse—a slow death."

"Hush and be nice, for a change."

"Ruff, go to hell."

When they trotted into the yard leading their Thoroughbred mares, Aunt Maybelle clapped her chubby little hands together with joy. "I do declare, I was afraid that you were all dead!"

Ruff dismounted and hugged his aunt. She was a short, plump woman with a flawless complexion and beautiful, china blue eyes. Once she was said to be the prettiest girl in all of Tennessee, and when Uncle Sid had taken her away, she became the prettiest bride in Mississippi. In a matronly, porcelain kind of way, Aunt Maybelle remained doll-like.

"My, my! What a surprise to see you three! I've been wondering for months how you and your father and brothers have been getting along over there at Wildwood."

Ruff looked at Houston. "You didn't tell her anything?"

"No time."

Aunt Maybelle was just about to hug Dixie but now her smile died. "Do declare, what are you boys talking about?"

"Pa is dead," Ruff said, trying to swallow his irritation at Houston for not breaking this terrible news. "So is John, Micha, and Mason. Us and these horses is all that is left."

Aunt Maybelle's eyes brimmed with tears and she plunged forward, arms outstretched to bury her face against Houston's broad chest. Houston looked helpless as his aunt had a good, long cry. Dixie took her horse over to the barn and began to unsaddle. Ruff didn't quite know what to do, so he just stood by and waited out the tears.

"You boys are all there is left?" Aunt Maybelle finally sniffled, looking forlornly up the road they'd just traveled as if she expected Justin or one of the others to come galloping over the rise.

"Don't forget Dixie," Ruff said, turning to motion toward his sister. "Pa's dying request was that you teach her how to act like a lady."

"That girl will *never* be a lady!" Aunt Maybelle cried, mopping her tears dry with a silk handkerchief. "She's still horse crazy, isn't she?"

"Yeah, but so are we. It runs deep in the Ballou family."

"It becomes a man to be a horseman, but not a woman," Maybelle said sternly. "Dixie is old enough to know that by now. She's what, twelve or thirteen?"

"Fourteen."

"Why, at fourteen I was already a debutante! I had young men of fine breeding flocking over to win my hand. At fifteen, I could boast three excellent marriage proposals!"

"Dixie doesn't even like men," Ruff explained. "Except for Houston and me."

"She's a lost cause," Aunt Maybelle lamented. "There is no hope for that girl."

Ruff looked to Houston for some support, but there was none forthcoming. Houston was still wallowing in his own self-pity and Ruff didn't know how much more of it he could stand.

"Aunt Maybelle, it was Pa's dying wish that you teach Dixie how to be a lady."

"Humpph! Well, it's like you horsemen are wont to say: You can lead a horse to water, but you can't make the fool thing drink."

Ruff had to grin a little. "That's true enough," he said, "but Dixie isn't a horse. Besides, I promised that she'd only have to stay here a month before I came back for her. Just a month. Aunt Maybelle, you two can be civil to each other for just a month, can't you?"

"I can be civil to anyone for that long, but what about her?"

"We've talked. She's agreed to the bargain."

"Very well. Perhaps something will rub off on her before she leaves. How to set a proper table, how to receive a guest, how to curtsy."

"I'd forget that curtsy business," Ruff suggested. "By the way, have you had any Yank patrols pass through?"

"Of course. I charmed their socks off. I have nothing to fear from those boys."

Her comment roused a fire in Houston's eyes and Ruff saw hard words coming. He headed them off by allowing High Man to get too close to Houston's young stallion. The old horse nipped his offspring and the two Thoroughbreds squealed and struck at each other.

"Dammit, Ruff," Houston shouted, pulling his young stallion back, "don't be so careless!"

"Sorry." Ruff remounted High Man. "Aunt Maybelle, we'll stable these stallions in your barn, then come back and visit."

"Do that. All my slaves ran off with the Union soldiers but I can still make some lovely lemonade for you."

"Good," Ruff said, realizing how weary he was after all the adventures and narrow escapes they'd had since leaving their beloved Tennessee horse farm.

After they reached the barn, Ruff glanced over at Houston. "I'd suggest you just keep your thoughts about the Yankee soldiers to yourself. It's clear that Aunt Maybelle has made some kind of a truce with them."

"If they gallop up that road," Houston said, patting his holster, "I'll give them a hell of a lot more than a 'deal.' I'll give them hot lead!"

Ruff clamped his own mouth shut. It was abundantly clear that keeping the peace between Dixie, Aunt Maybelle, and Houston was going to be a full-time chore.

They stayed almost a week and by then both Ruff and Houston were too restless to remain any longer at Aunt Maybelle's plantation. To her credit, Dixie was putting on her best face and trying to be polite and mannerly. She spent her mornings with the horses and then, her spirit bolstered, she gave her afternoons and evenings over to Aunt Maybelle's long, preachy lectures on etiquette and the life-style expected of a Southern lady.

Ruff watched Dixie as she was forced to listen to such nonsense and he felt an overwhelming sense of guilt and pity. Dixie would nod her head, even murmur some little comment to indicate that she was listening, but Ruff knew better. Dixie's mind was out the door and either back to Wildwood Farm or to her beloved Thoroughbreds.

On the morning they left, Dixie looked so depressed that Ruff took her aside for a minute and said, "One week is passed, so there's just three to go. You can do it!"

"I *have* to do it," Dixie said morosely. "And I will, even if it kills me."

"It might do you good."

"More likely it'll kill me."

Ruff could see that it was as useless to try to cheer Dixie up as it was Houston. Both of them were acting as if they were about to be drawn and quartered. That being the case, he said good-bye to his sister and aunt, then mounted High Man.

"Three weeks," Dixie said before he and Houston rode away. "Three weeks or I'm on my way to the Indian Territory!"

"She means it," Houston said.

"I know. And I'll keep my part of the bargain. What about you?"

"I don't care," Houston muttered without interest. "I don't care about much of anything."

"Well, dammit," Ruff said in anger, "you'd better *start* caring!"

Houston looked at him but the tone of Ruff's voice didn't even anger him. It was as if, when he'd lost Molly O'Day, he'd lost all interest in life.

Two days passed like two years for Dixie. She tried and tried to be pleasant and sociable, but Aunt Maybelle's constant lectures and carping about how to set a table, dress, and care for your hands and hair were about to send Dixie into fits. So it was that when a group of five ragged deserters appeared, Dixie almost welcomed the dangerous company.

Aunt Maybelle didn't. When she saw the scarecrow men coming toward her house, she nearly had a stroke. "My God, we've got to run them off! They're not to be trusted!"

Dixie found her father's gun and also the Colt that Ruff had left for their protection. "Just keep calm. Probably all they want is some food and they'll continue along on their way."

"Are they Southern boys, or Yanks?"

"Johnny Rebs," Dixie said.

Aunt Maybelle was so nervous and upset that she looked ready to swoon. "I can deal with real soldiers on either side," she fretted out loud. "But all the terrible outrages I hear about are due to deserters. They're the ones that have no authority or conscience. They're dishonorable men, Dixie!"

"Why don't you go inside," Dixie suggested. "I'll deal with them."

"You're just a girl!"

"That's right," Dixie said, "and so maybe they'll leave me be and go away."

Aunt Maybelle rushed into the house. Dixie waited, aware of the hard stares that she was receiving from the approaching deserters.

"Well, well," a man said in a hoarse voice, "if it isn't Miss Dixie Ballou!"

Dixie stared. The man who addressed her was vaguely familiar. He wore moccasins and a dirty red bandanna was wrapped around his throat. His narrow face was covered by a scraggly beard, and his long, muscular legs were wrapped in buckskin.

"Do I know you?"

"We've met," he said. "My name was Lieutenant Pike."

Dixie trembled. Her voice took on a cutting edge and she lifted her pistol. "Of course! You murdered my father!"

Pike nodded and his expression was ugly. "That's right, and your brother Rufus shot me in the throat. I almost bled to death on the road. Would have if the ball had gone a hair deeper."

The pistol in Dixie's fist began to shake violently. "Get out of here!"

"Boys," Pike said, "fan out and let's declaw this little tiger!"

Dixie pulled the trigger as fast as she could, not even bothing to aim. Pike yelped and men went flying in all directions. Dixie spun and ran into the house.

"Aunt Maybelle!"

"Oh, dear God!" the woman cried. "Now they'll kill us both!"

Dixie glanced back toward the front yard. "I'm sorry," she rushed, "but they would have killed me anyway. We have to get to the woods and hide."

"No!"

"But there's no choice!"

"There is always a choice," Aunt Maybelle declared. "And I will not abandon my home to that filth!"

Dixie knew she had only one chance to save herself, and that was to run for help. "Then I'm going to get Ruff and Houston. I'll be back as soon as I can!"

She turned and started to run for the back door. "Stall them for me, Aunt Maybelle. Those I didn't kill, tell them I'm hiding upstairs!"

Aunt Maybelle fainted right in her own hallway, but Dixie didn't have time to help her for she was already bolting out the back door. Her plan was to circle through the woods and get her hands on one of the mares. If she could do that, she had a chance.

My God, she wondered, how far ahead are Ruff and Houston?

SEVENTEEN

If it hadn't been for High Man throwing a shoe and going lame near Holly Springs, Ruff and Houston would have been across the wide Mississippi River before Dixie overtook them. As it was, she could scarcely believe her good fortune as she galloped up to the pair of big men on their tall horses.

"Ruff!" she cried. "Houston!"

Both twisted around in their saddles, but when Ruff saw her coming, he swore in anger. "Dammit, she *promised* she'd stay with Aunt Maybelle three more weeks! She broke her word!"

Houston studied Dixie and his eyes detected the weariness in both the horse and rider. "I think there's trouble," he said, snapping out of his lethargy. "Otherwise, Dixie wouldn't ride a pregnant mare that hard."

The minute his brother made that comment, Ruff knew Houston was right. Something was *very* wrong.

They both waited until Dixie drew in her badly winded mare. "I shot some deserters," she blurted. "They were going to hurt me so I opened fire on the bunch of them and ran for my life."

"How many?" Houston demanded, coming alive at long last.

"Lieutenant Pike and a bunch more. I'd say eight or nine altogether."

Ruff was astonished. "The man that killed Pa and that I shot in the throat? *That* Lieutenant Pike?"

Dixie nodded. "He's like a ghost! And his voice, it's . . . it's terrible."

Ruff dismounted. He yanked his saddle off the mare he was riding and threw it on one of the young stallions. High Man had been shod, but he was still too tenderfooted to be raced all the way back to Aunt Maybelle's.

"I'm coming with you," Houston said, preparing to transfer his saddle to the other young stallion.

"What about me?" Dixie wailed.

Ruff looked at her. "You're going to have to bring along these Thoroughbreds. It's all up to you, Dixie. We'll go on ahead and see what we can do for Aunt Maybelle."

"How many deserters were left standing after you opened fire?" Houston asked.

"I don't know! The smoke was so thick and . . . well, I just ran for the house! I never bothered to wait around and keep score."

"You abandoned Aunt Maybelle?"

"Of course not! I tried to make her escape into the woods with me, but she wouldn't do it. She's got more sand in her craw than I ever gave her credit for, I'll say that much. Said she wasn't about to abandon her home to such filth."

Ruff exchanged worried glances with his brother. Aunt Maybelle had her faults, but she was their father's sister and she was made of the same unbending iron. She would stand up and fight before she'd back down.

Ruff finished changing saddles and then bridles. "Houston, are you ready?"

"Yeah," Houston said, jamming the Spencer rifle into a scabbard. "Let's ride!"

"Dixie, watch out for Union patrols!" Ruff called as he raced away. "This country is crawling with them!"

The three-year-olds were thin and weary, but they were game and plenty ready to run. In fact, the trick was in holding them down to a pace that would sustain them back to Aunt Maybelle's little tobacco plantation without breaking down their joints, hooves, or tendons. Ruff set the pace and it consisted of fifteen minutes of alternating between an extended gallop and a trot. He kept his eyes trained on his stallion, noting its respiration rate and its general state of condition. He could also sense its "solidness" with each stride and he'd know the instant it began to falter.

An exhausted horse was more inclined to stumble, and its head would droop along with its ears. But as long as its ears were pricked up and forward, and its head was high and its stride long and smooth, Ruff knew his valiant Thoroughbred stallion was standing up to the brutal pace.

It had been two days since leaving Aunt Maybelle's plantation but that was partially because High Man had gone lame and they'd been so wary of stumbling into a Union patrol. Now, on younger, sound horses and with the fear of a Union patrol secondary to the safety of Aunt Maybelle, Ruff figured that he and Houston could reach their aunt in less than fourteen hours.

"Wish we had a couple relay mounts!" he yelled to his brother. "We'd be able to cut the time down to ten or twelve hours."

"Either way," Houston said, "Aunt Maybelle might still be a goner."

"If she is, we'll track down those that killed her and finish them off before we leave Mississippi."

Houston dipped his chin in agreement. His backbone had straightened and his shoulders were thrown back. He was looking good on a horse again and there was a light in his eyes that had not been there since he'd said good-bye to Molly.

All evening long the Ballou men rode at a relentless pace, and when the stars came out in their full glory, they used them to guide their way eastward. Once they almost ran into a Union patrol, but as luck would have it, they had pulled their weary stallions off the road so that they could slake their thirsts in a clear meadow stream. At about three o'clock in the morning, two drunken men opened fire on them from the darkest shadows of the forest. Ruff and Houston did not bother to return fire but kept moving eastward.

Dawn found them close enough to Aunt Maybelle's plantation that they could see the rising sun bathe Mississippi's tallest peak with liquid gold.

"Are we going to simply gallop into the yard shooting at anything that moves, or do we need a plan?" Ruff shouted.

"Who needs a plan?"

"Maybe we do! There aren't going to be any second chances."

But Houston shook his head in anger. He drew his Spencer rifle and it was clear from his expression that he was going to throw caution to the wind. Ruff swore to himself. There was no help for it, he was also going to have to charge headlong into whatever awaited them.

"At least let's break from the road and cut through the woods so we can be upon them in a hurry!" Ruff yelled at his brother.

Before Houston could think of a reason why this was not a worthy idea, Ruff reined his stallion through the trees. Houston swore but he followed and, together, they raced headlong through the forest. Ruff picked up a game trail that snaked through the worst of the brush and fallen trees, and it brought him right out into the yard less than seventy yards from Aunt Maybelle's mansion.

Six unkempt deserters were reclining on the veranda, and when they saw Ruff and Houston atop the lathered Thoroughbreds, they gaped and clawed for their weapons.

Ruff's pistol was already in his fist. He opened fire at forty yards, knowing he'd miss because he was on horseback. But his bullet shattered a big plate-glass window behind the six and caused them to panic. Houston's bullets were adding to the mayhem, and then one of his slugs found the mark. A man clutched his chest and crashed over a chair, dead before he struck the porch.

Ruff fired twice more, and though he missed again, splinters erupted from the porch rail and speared one of the deserters. The ex-soldier hollered and covered what had been his eye. A second later, another of Houston's bullets caused him to flop over the porch rail, cutting his cry short, as though with scissors.

Two of the men panicked and ran for their lives.

"I'll get 'em!" Houston bellowed, taking off after the pair and emptying his rifle before tossing it aside and bringing another man down with his pistol. The last man escaped and disappeared into the forest, running like a thing gone wild.

Bullets were still flying and Ruff felt his horse stagger. Instinctively, he kicked out of the stirrups as the young stallion's head dropped and the animal began to somersault. Ruff slammed to earth, rolled through Aunt Maybelle's rose garden, tearing his flesh, and came to a halt beside the veranda. He heard more gunshots and dragged his bloody fist up to realize he had a man in his gunsights.

"You!" Ruff cried at the tall, ferret-faced man swaying above him.

Pike was already half-dead, thanks to Dixie. His torso was heavily bandaged and his face was twisted with hatred as he raised a pistol. The gun belched fire and smoke. Ruff twitched as a bullet fired from above nicked his hip, cutting neatly through the leather of his belt.

"I told 'em all you killed Captain Denton and shot your own people!" Pike shrieked as he struggled to cock the hammer of his six-gun. "The name Ballou has become a curse in the South!"

Ruff shot the son of a bitch between the eyes.

Pike disappeared backward through the shattered plate-glass window.

Ruff heard a horse squeal in terror somewhere behind him. He turned around to see Houston dismount on the run and then kneel by the wounded stallion's side. One look at Houston's face told Ruff that the horse was finished.

"Shoot him!"

Houston put the muzzle of his Colt to the stallion's head and fired. The horse jerked spasmodically. Its legs thrashed about and its hide burned. Houston shot the dying animal again and the stallion went limp.

Houston climbed to his feet and his steps were wooden as he crossed the yard and then reached down to his brother. "You all right?"

"I think I'm a lot better than I look," Ruff said, coming to his feet.

"Let's find out if Aunt Maybelle is still alive."

Ruff used his sleeve to wipe thorns and blood from his face, and then climbed up on the porch and walked over to the shot-out window to stare at Pike.

"I wish I'd have killed him the first time," Ruff said, climbing through the window and starting down the hallway.

"Aunt Maybelle! Aunt Maybelle! It's Rufus and Houston! Can you hear me!"

They both heard her screech with defiance and they rushed the stairs. Aunt Maybelle was on the second-floor landing, a pistol clenched in her small, chubby fists. She looked a little crazy but damned determined to shoot anything attempting to mount the stairs.

"Don't shoot us, for heaven's sake!" Houston ordered. "Not after all that we've been through!"

She dropped the pistol and came flying down the stairs like a spring chicken. She threw herself into Houston's arms and he hugged her tight.

"You dear, dear handsome man!" she cried. "You've come to save me!"

"We *both* did," Houston said, trying to disengage himself from her stranglehold.

Aunt Maybelle broke away and really looked at Ruff for the first time. "Dear heavens!" she whispered, and then fainted again.

Houston and Ruff were too exhausted to react fast enough to keep Maybelle from hitting the floor. Ruff shook his head. "Can you believe this, Houston? After all she's been through, *now* she faints."

"And she isn't even faking," Houston said with amazement as he squatted down on his bootheels to pat the old lady's plump apple cheeks. "Why, I hear tell that when she was a debutante, she could swoon at the bat of an eyelash."

"Is that a fact?"

"Yep. She did it constantly and always made sure that she landed in some handsome young gentleman's arms."

"Well," Ruff said, turning to gaze outside, "what do we do now?"

"We wait for Dixie."

"But then we ride," Ruff said. "We're going to take the last of our horses and live with our mother's people, the Cherokee."

Houston's eyes grew distant, and Ruff could tell he was thinking about Washington, D.C., and Molly O'Day.

"She'll come back," Ruff said, laying his hand on Houston's shoulder. "And she'll find you wherever we go."

"Yeah," Houston said distantly, "so we'll take the last of our horses West."

That suited Ruff just fine. There was no looking back now. Not to Wildwood Farm or to the closed doors of their gentried Southern past. There was only today and maybe a tomorrow. Ruff guessed that was all any man really had when you got right down to the hard, naked truth.